R26   ⊙ 7/98   W9
                                                    9 1

MAIN

SPECIAL MESSAGE TO READERS

This book is published under the auspices of

THE ULVERSCROFT FOUNDATION

(registered charity No. 264873 UK)

Established in 1972 to provide funds for research, diagnosis and treatment of eye diseases. Examples of contributions made are: —

A new Children's Assessment Unit at Moorfield's Hospital, London.

•

Twin operating theatres at the Western Ophthalmic Hospital, London.

•

A Chair of Ophthalmology at the University of Leicester.

•

The establishment of a Royal Australian College of Ophthalmologists "Fellowship".

You can help further the work of the Foundation by making a donation or leaving a legacy. Every contribution, no matter how small, is received with gratitude. Please write for details to:

**THE ULVERSCROFT FOUNDATION,
The Green, Bradgate Road, Anstey,
Leicester LE7 7FU, England.
Telephone: (0116) 236 4325**

**In Australia write to:
THE ULVERSCROFT FOUNDATION,
c/o The Royal Australian College of
Ophthalmologists,
27, Commonwealth Street, Sydney,
N.S.W. 2010.**

THE WEST WITCH

A fatal mistake ended the Black Hood Bandits' murderous spree. When east coast detective Quinton Hilcrest journeys west seeking the bandits' lost fortune, he finds the Black Hood legacy alive in the town of Hags Bend. Within hours he is fighting for his life, ensnared with a vengeful bargirl — and a beautiful outcast the town claims is a witch! Can he save the young woman from the angry mob? Or will he be caught in the spell of the west witch?

Books by Lance Howard
in the Linford Western Library:

THE COMANCHE'S GHOST

LANCE HOWARD

THE WEST WITCH

Complete and Unabridged

LINFORD
Leicester

First published in Great Britain in 1995 by
Robert Hale Limited
London

First Linford Edition
published 1997
by arrangement with
Robert Hale Limited
London

British Library CIP Data

Hopkins, Lance
    The west witch.—Large print ed.—
Linford western library
    1. English fiction—20th century
    2. Large type books
    I. Title
    823.9′14 [F]

ISBN 0–7089–7989–0

Published by
F. A. Thorpe (Publishing) Ltd.
Anstey, Leicestershire
Set by Words & Graphics Ltd.
Anstey, Leicestershire
Printed and bound in Great Britain by
T. J. Press (Padstow) Ltd., Padstow, Cornwall

For
Paul Ernst and
Richard Henry Benson
& the gang!

1

THE window of the Casper Ridge bank exploded, spewing debris into the dusty street. Shards of glass, glittering with captured sunlight, spiralled to the boardwalk. Plumes of smoke billowed from the interior. The building shimmied, shuddered, appearing as if it would collapse.

"Judas Priest!" blurted a man in a black hood, as he straightened from behind a water trough across the street. Through eye slits, brown eyes narrowing, he shot a look at a second black-hooded man. "You used a galldamned 'nough of that dynamite, didncha?"

The second man shrugged, swivelling his gaze to the bank, back to his partner, shrugging again.

"You damn near blew the whole building down!" the first continued,

1

jabbing a finger at the bank. "Fat lot of good that woulda done us, now, wouldn't it?"

"Won't do us a lick a good standin' here jawin' 'bout a misreckon, will it? Jess get our necks stretched."

The first man grunted, but seemed to agree.

As if choreographed, the men slid from their positions. The second bandit scuttled in a crouch across the street while easing a Colt from the holster at his hip and thumbing back the hammer. The first man followed a beat behind, drawing his iron.

The bandits were garbed in faded trousers and washed-out blue shirts. Stetsons dipped low on their foreheads, over black hoods tied at the neck. The hoods concealed their features except for slits cut at the eyes and nostrils. Besides masking their identities, the hoods gave them a menacing presence.

The rubble settled, leaving the bank standing — barely. The silence following the blast seemed crushing. Few townsfolk populated the wide main street as the early-morning sun glazed the buildings with honey-coloured light. The few who did took one look at the bank and fled, dashing for their homes or horses.

The bandits paused at the bank doorway, peering in. Within the lobby an iron-haired man was gaining his feet behind a desk. Two tellers peeked over the counter behind the cage; a woman, the first customer of the day, was shrieking.

"Want I should throw another stick?" the second bandit asked, voice hopeful as he glanced at the two sticks of dynamite tucked into his gunbelt.

"And blow us all to hell, along with the money? Are you loco or just plain stupid?"

"You shouldn't oughta talk to me like that, Cal. You know I don't like it none. Makes me wanna blow somethin' up!"

"Judas Priest! You are loco! Don't use my name. And don't get no crazy notions 'bout blowin' anything else.

3

That almost got our necks stretched in Cheyenne!"

"We do any more talkin' 'bout it and we'll likely get 'em stretched here!"

The first bandit nodded his agreement and burst into the bank, waving his Colt. "Giddown, all of ya and no one'll get dead!"

The iron-haired man, the bank manager according to the tipped-over nameplate on his desk, took on a look of terror and dropped behind the desk. The tellers jerked their hands ceilingward, frightened expressions jumping on to their faces. The woman kept shrieking.

"Shaddup!" Cal, the first bandit, shouted at her, swinging his gun. The woman seemed not to hear; her voice notched upward in shrillness.

"Judas Priest!" Cal blurted, levelling his Colt and triggering a shot.

As the gun centered on her, the woman's eyes widened and her scream chopped short. She fainted, collapsing into a heap on the wooden floor. The faint saved her life. The bullet, fired a split second behind, whined through the space her head had occupied and burrowed into a wall.

The hooded bandit shot her a glance and ran to the teller cage, jabbing his Colt at one of the men.

"You start fillin' a sack with money or you'll be swallowin' the lead she just missed . . ."

The teller stammered a nod and snatched up a canvas bag from the corner. As he began stuffing bills into it, the second teller watched in frozen terror.

"What the hell you lookin' at?" Cal asked. "You're makin' me antsy."

The teller struggled to speak, mouth making fish movements, but no words coming out. Sweat dribbled down his forehead and his eyelids fluttered.

"Aw hell!" the bandit muttered, raising his Colt. "I hate cowards . . ." He triggered a shot. The blast shuddered through the room like demons laughing. A red blotch ripened on the teller's white shirt. He looked down, stunned, disbelieving, then pitched backward to the floor. His body spasmed, went rigid.

During the incident, the second bandit moved to the vault, grabbing a canvas bag on the way. He stepped into the chamber, dashing out a few seconds later, bag half-filled.

"Hey, there ain't hardly nothin' here!" Disappointment laced his voice, along with an edge of anger. He whirled on the iron-haired man, prodding his Colt towards him. "Where's the money, rust-head?"

"It — it's all we have!" the man stammered, spittle flecking his lips. "Things haven't been so good lately, wrong day for deposits . . . " The iron-haired man looked up with dancing eyelids, a plea staining his face.

"Reckon things just got a whole lot worse . . . " The black-hooded bandit drew a stick of dynamite from his belt and holstered his gun. Striking a lucifer, he touched it to the wick. The sparkling light, eating its way along the fuse, appeared to fascinate the bandit as he stared dreamily at it. It burned down, halfway, three-quarters . . .

"Hey, you damn fool!" Cal yelled, turning in the second bandit's direction.

The yell snapped the second man's daze and he flung the dynamite at the iron-haired man.

The bank manager bleated, tried to scramble out of the way. The dynamite rolled after him as if attached.

The second bandit dived towards the first and they pitched for cover.

The dynamite exploded.

The percussion was deafening. The desk disintegrated in a shower of wood and smoke. Slivers stung the bandits, followed by red raindrops — blood! The iron-haired man vanished beneath a hail of desk parts and floorboards thrown up as the explosion gouged a crater into the floor. His family would have little to bury.

"Judas Priest!" screeched Cal. "I can't hear a galldamned thing!"

The second bandit glared at Cal with an almost maniacal glaze in his eyes.

Behind the counter, the teller pushed himself off the floor and Cal darted for him, snatching the money bag, partially filled, from his grip.

"This all of it?"

The teller jerked a nod.

"Ain't much — Judas Priest!" His gaze narrowed on the teller. "Here's somethin' to recollect us by." He raised his Colt as the teller whirled to run. A blast sounded and the teller jumped in mid-stride, skipping a pace across the room and slamming into a table. He slid to the floor, blood pooling beneath him.

"Let's skedaddle!" Cal lined for the door.

"What about her?" the second bandit asked, hauling the sack and pointing to the fainted woman.

"Leave her. She ain't seen nothin' 'cept these masks and she can spread the word the Black Hood Bandits paid their fair town a visit."

The men raced through the door out into the street. They scooted for their horses, tethered in an alley a few blocks down.

A commotion had commenced in the street. Folks were poking their heads out of windows, screaming about the bank being robbed. A few brave individuals ventured outside, gawking. Cal whirled and blasted shots in their direction, sending them scurrying back into buildings.

Four blocks down, a door opened and a portly sheriff stumbled from his office, wiping sleep out of his eyes and buckling on his gunbelt. His gaze centered on the bandits as he skipped along the boardwalk, pulling a Peacemaker and shouting; "Stop or I'll shoot!"

Cal laughed, sending a volley of lead in the lawman's direction. The sheriff dived behind a trough, but not before a bullet burrowed into his arm.

The bandits reached their horses, leaping into saddles and reining around after securing the moneybags.

They thundered out of town, triggering lead behind them to discourage followers.

★ ★ ★

Butter-colored lantern-light fluttered from the stone walls of a vaulted room. It blended with the darkness to create marble shadows. Moisture seeped from the walls, gleaming black in the pale light, as if the walls dripped blood. The place carried a stench, a stench that suggested things decaying, but Cal tried to force that thought out of his mind. If he dwelled on it for too long, he'd get the creeps and from there it was a short walk to loco.

Cal's face was craggy, showing more wear than any twenty-five-year-old face should have shown. At his forearm lay a crumpled black hood. He glanced at the man sitting across from him at the rickety wooden table. The other a notch older, sporting a semi-blank expression that told Cal his partner

10

might have already stepped over the line, that he was plumb loco in the worst way — the subtle way that made men do strange things, though you couldn't outright tell they were nuts. That worried him.

The other man looked up from the stack of cash he'd finished counting, a disgruntled look twisting his lips. "Galldamn! We only come away with a few hunnert dollars, mostly small bills. We sure picked a damn fine bank to rob!"

Cal focused on his partner, studying his expression in the lantern light. He shivered inside. Maybe it was just this chamber they had picked for a headquarters or maybe it was the knowledge that sooner or later his partner would pull a boner with dynamite that would end their robberies and their lives. The chamber was a necessity: it afforded them the sanctuary they needed, furnished them with their reputation of being black-hooded ghosts that vanished into the very air. A necessity, but still it ate at his innards, gave him a feeling he was in hell for all his crimes and the only thing needed to complete the illusion was to have the Devil ride up and join them for beans.

The second thing, John, his partner, he could do something about, though he admitted it had to be carried out in a subtle way. A slight fear gnawed at him when it came to John, as if he never quite knew whether his partner would slip off the edge completely and decide he wanted everything for himself. That had to be dealt with. And he reckoned what he had in mind would do it.

"You damn near got us caught today, John," Cal said evenly, pulling out the makings and rolling a smoke.

John grunted, reached for the open whiskey bottle resting on the table next to a stick of dynamite. "Don't sweat it, pard. I was just funnin' a bit."

Cal blew a scoffing grunt. "Funnin'? You keep funnin' that way and we'll be meetin' St Peter himself."

"Ain't much chance of that." John swigged a gulp from the whiskey bottle. "We got us a room all reserved at the Brimstone Hotel and it won't be no saint welcomin' us."

"You gotta get control of yourself." Cal's eyes narrowed as he locked with the other man's gaze. "I figure our luck is close to runnin' out with this thing anyhow."

"What the hell's that s'posed to mean? We got the best thing goin'. We're like ghosts — papers all say so. Black-hooded demons from hell who jess ride in an' vanish into thin air. We won't never get caught."

"Not with what I'm plannin'."

John cocked an eyebrow. "Yeah? What you fixin' on?"

Cal groped in his pocket and drew out a section of folded newspaper, tossing it in front of the other man.

"You know I cain't read a lick. Tell me what it says."

Cal chuckled, the admission by his

partner giving him a small measure of satisfaction. He figured it made him one step better than John, one step farther away from insanity.

"Says there's a stage comin' into Hags Bend tomorrah, lickety-split early."

"So what? Stage comes in there all the time. A little nothin' town. Nothin' important's gonna be on it."

"That's where you're wrong. Got me the inside scoop on it. Everybody knows Hags Bend's a nothin' town and nobody in their right mind would send anything through it — leastwise not nothin' important enough to steal."

"But . . . ?"

"But I happened to find out there's gonna be a big stash of jewels on it; diamonds big as robin's eggs, I hear tell. Maybe emeralds, sapphires, too."

"Maybe? You best be sure 'bout somethin' like that, Cal."

Cal eyed his partner, wondering about his incongruously good judgement, then dismissing it, unable to fathom the man.

"I'm galldamn sure. It'll be the biggest haul of our lives — and the last."

"What the hell you talkin' 'bout, the last?"

"Just what I said. This'll make us so rich we'll never have to risk our hides again. We'll be livin' it, John, the lap of luxury and no more worries."

John's gaze lowered to the table. He seemed to drift into his own world for dragging moments. His gaze lifted to his partner. "I like it, least the jewel part. But I ain't so sure I want to retire. I kinda enjoy what I do. Ain't got the smarts for nothin' else."

"Fair 'nough. After we get the jewels we split half and half. Me, I'm all set for a life of ease. You, well, you got your choice to do whatever you want."

An unreadable look crossed John's eyes and Cal didn't like it one bit. It meant the unspoken part of his plan had to go into action after the robbery. Because the look said his partner didn't

15

want to end their little operation and that included *both* of them. He was right when he said he didn't have the smarts for anything else, and knew he would need Cal to survive after the robbery.

That's where the second part of the plan came in. This chamber would make a perfect burial room . . .

John picked up the stick of dynamite, turning it over in his hand, sliding his fingers over the rough surface. "You got the details?"

"Don't I always?" Cal grinned a fake grin.

John gave an equally wooden nod and snatched up the whiskey bottle. "Here's to retirement." A note of grimness hung in his voice.

★ ★ ★

As the sun scorched the landscape with brass light, a stage rattled along the hard-packed trail leading into Hags Bend. A mile distant, the drivers saw

16

the town rise into view and felt a twinge of relief, knowing they had reached their destination and could unload the cargo burdening their coach and their minds. Heavily armed with Winchesters and Colts, the two men were prepared for the worst, though they prayed it would never come. Why should it? No one knew about the shipment, save for a few folks involved and the lawyer handling the estate. Jewels, a hoard of them, glittering with sparkles of variegated light — diamonds, rubies, sapphires and emeralds, all willed to some woman in California by an eastern uncle. Worth somewhere north of a million dollars, imbued with an air of nitroglycerin. They feared at any moment some hardcase would spring from the trailside and start blasting. But that was next to impossible with the security employed in carrying the shipment. The operation was airtight; they had no cause to be boogered.

Did they?

Something felt just plain wrong.

Something swelling in the air like the brewing of a blizzard. A smell, a taste, a *feeling*.

"Tellin' you, ain't nothin' to fret about, Jasper," one of the guards said, glancing at his partner, who kept an eye on the forest-flanked trail for any hint of something askew.

"I know, Hank. Jest call me superstitious, but I got a notion I smell skunk somewhere."

"The word's 'paranoid'." Hank chuckled, a hint of nervousness creeping into his humor.

"Oh, yeah . . . " Jasper nodded, a trickle of sweat dribbling down his forehead.

Hank shifted in his seat. "What you worried about? No one could possibly know 'bout the jewels and once we get to Hags Bend we'll unload them on the bank there. Their problem after that. Lookee, the town's right yonder. Ain't a thing in this world that could go wrong — "

A shot shattered the peaceful morning.

18

For an instant, both men froze, too stunned by the suddenness of the blast to react.

"*Jumpin'* — " Jasper blurted, swinging his Winchester up and levering a shell into the chamber. "I told ya! I told ya!"

"Shaddup, you galldamned fool and do your job!" Hank bleated. He struggled with the horses, which had been boogered by the shot. The stage jounced, lurched, careened forward. He fought the reins, as Jasper swung the rifle in every direction, unable to pinpoint where the shot had come from.

He didn't have to.

Two men bolted into view, blocking the trail. They were bold, the thought struck Hank, real bold, to meet the stage so close to town. Another thing hit him in an instant of plunging dread and he gasped, "Godamighty, it's them Black Hoods the papers been rantin' about!"

"Shoot the varmints!" Jasper yelled,

19

as Hank managed to control the horses.

Jasper brought up the Winchester, levelling it on the first outlaw.

The second bandit's arm cocked, flashed forward. An object tumbled through the air, hit the trail in front of them.

Jasper fired. His shot went wide and he got no chance to trigger another.

An explosion threw up huge chunks of earth before them; a shower of dirt and sticks peltered their bodies. The concussion shattered Jasper's eardrums. The horses, only feet from the blast, collapsed, unmoving. The stage slammed to a halt, canted. Jasper and Hank tumbled from the seat, crashing to the ground.

"Dynamite!" Hank yelled, though Jasper could no longer hear him.

The stage creaked, moaned, fell on its side. The door popped open and two more guards, rifles in hand, clambered out. Half-stunned, they aimed their rifles.

Two shots blasted from the bandits'

guns. The guards flew backward off the stage, one missing a portion of his face, the other gouting blood from a hole in his chest.

Jasper gained his feet, Hank grabbing his arm and helping him up.

"Come on, Jasp! We ain't got no chance. Let's git. Let 'em have the galldamned jewels!"

Hank began to run, but Jasper, whether from bravery or terror, stood stock still, jerking up his rifle as the bandits charged for him. The move came too late. The outlaws' guns came level, pumped lead.

Jasper did a morbid dance, red blotches ripening on his chest. A glazed look stained his eyes. He crumpled to the ground, unmoving.

A volley of lead followed the fleeing guard, but Hank managed to escape by dashing into the woods and not stopping to look back.

"Ooo-wee!" the first bandit yelled, leaping from his horse. He scooted over to Jasper, surveyed the other dead guards, then turned to John, who trotted up behind him. "Looks like they won't be puttin' in for no pension. Damn shame!" Cal laughed.

"Told you the dynamite would stop 'em." A strange sense of pride hung on John's words. "Next time you'll listen to me more, woncha?"

Cal turned away, making sure no betrayal of what he was thinking showed on his face. "Yeah . . . next time . . . "

They went to the stage and climbed atop. Leaning in, Cal located the strongbox and heaved it up, passing it to John, who stood straddle-legged across the door opening.

"Get the sack," Cal ordered as John set the box down. "The box is too heavy to haul."

John complied, running back to his horse and grabbing one of the canvas bags from the bank robbery the previous day. "Here," he said, handing it to Cal, who, with a gloved hand, scooped a glimmering array of jewels into the bag.

"Look at them babies!" John's eyes

took on the same hypnotized glaze they did when he peered at his dynamite.

Cal nodded, barely able to contain his own enthusiasm. "Ain't nothin' gonna stop us now, pard! We done pulled our last job . . . "

★ ★ ★

Sheriff Bill Presby lowered himself into the seat behind his desk and heaved a sigh. A stocky man in his late forties, he had piercing grey eyes and a rugged face with a jaw like an anvil. He sipped at a steaming cup of Arbuckle's and spread a newspaper open on the desk. He scanned the headlines, shaking his head.

"What's it say?" asked the deputy named Justin, who sat in the chair across the room. The deputy turned a block of wood over in his hand and carved a long shred from it with a pocket knife. He was younger than Presby by about fifteen years, face freckled and flat.

Presby glanced over, a disgusted look ticking his face. "Says the Black Hood Bandits struck again."

"Where this time?"

"Casper Ridge, just south of here. Shot up a couple tellers and dynamited the bank manager. Let one woman live to tell the tale, though. That's been their habit."

"What'd they git?"

"Not much, I'll tell you. Misjudged the bank, it seems; only a few hundred, looks like. But they sure held to their reputation as brutal killers. A bit heavy on the dynamite this time, too. Damn bank had to be condemned."

"Casper Ridge ain't that far from here. Fact, none of the places they hit so far are. Reckon they could be headed our way?"

"Hell, we got less than Casper Ridge. Ain't much point to it. But they gotta be somewhere awfully close to here, I figure, way they always vanish like they was spooks."

"In town?"

The sheriff shrugged. "Maybe. Maybe not. Seems like a nowhere town like Hags Bend is as good as any to hole up while hitting more prosperous towns."

"No one's seen 'em . . . "

"Nope, no one has. They're clever *hombres*, but I see a pattern developin'."

"Yeah?" The deputy stopped whittling, interest glittering in his eyes.

"Noticed every account says they use more and more dynamite; too much for their purposes. I figure one of 'em's got some sort of fixation with it. That might give us some sort of advantage."

"You reckon?"

"Yep, I do. How, don't ask me. Jest have to wait and — "

The office door burst open and Sheriff Presby started. The deputy came straight in his chair and both men peered at the bedraggled man who stumbled in. The man was panting, stuttering something unintelligible.

Presby lifted out of his chair. Going to the man, he gripped the fellow's shoulders and shook him. "What in tarnation happened, fella? Calm down and tell me."

"I — I'm one of the guards on the stage comin' into town . . . " The man gasped for breath and shuddered. "They just clean held us up! They killed Jasper, killed 'em all!"

"Get ahold of yourself!" Presby shook the guard again. "Who held up the stage?"

"Them!" He jabbed a finger at the opened newspaper with glaring headlines. "The Black Hood Bandits!"

Presby's eyes widened, gaze jerking to the deputy, who rose, setting aside his whittling.

"God Almighty . . . what in hell were you carryin'?"

"Jewels! A million's worth — you gotta stop 'em!"

Presby guided the guard to a chair as his words turned into a babble. The guard collapsed into it, face in hands. Sobs wracked his body. Presby looked at the deputy who was already lifting rifles from a wall rack and checking loads.

"Looks like we'll have our chance at 'em." Grimness weighted Presby's tone.

"No one who has has come back to tell of it . . . " The deputy's face tightened.

"Let's hope we're the first." Presby grabbed a rifle and checked the chamber of his Peacemaker, making sure it was full. He walked out on to the boardwalk, trailed by the deputy. Mounting their horses, which were tethered to the rail outside the office, they reined around and gigged the animals into a gallop towards the opening of town. Presby had no trouble determining where the robbery occurred. Townsfolk were shouting, rushing about, pointing; Presby followed the ruckus.

They reached the stage within seconds and a glance told Presby all that had happened. Dead guards and horses, a huge hole blasted into the hardpack, the stage lying on its side. The calling cards of the Black Hood Bandits: dynamite and death. He shot the deputy a glance, whose face pinched at the sight of the carnage.

"Only one way they could go," Presby said, nodding down the trail. The deputy nodded, swallowing hard. Presby heeled his horse forward.

As he rode, he studied the trail ahead. He noticed a settling cloud of dust, disturbed trail dirt and knew he had figured right: the bandits couldn't be far ahead. He mumbled a prayer, knowing the odds were against them and they had to be at their best if they hoped to come out of this alive.

"There!" the deputy shouted beside him, jabbing a finger at a spot a hundred yards in front of them.

Presby's eyes narrowed. He saw them, two horses, two riders. The bandits' pace appeared leisurely, as if they expected no pursuit, especially from a nowhere town like Hags Bend.

That, Presby reckoned, might be just the advantage he needed.

He spurred his horse into a faster gait, the deputy following suit. The distance between them and the outlaws fell away in heartbeats.

"They seen us!" the deputy blurted.

One of the bandits had swivelled his head, as if some sixth sense had alerted him to the fact they were being dogged. The other glanced back, and Presby clearly saw the slits for eyes and nostrils in their black hoods.

"Just like the papers told it," he muttered, a wind of fear sweeping through his innards. This was his chance at the bandits the papers had dubbed 'unstoppable', his chance at bringing down the most vicious gang the area had ever seen. He gritted his teeth against the fear and pushed his horse harder, unlimbering his Peacemaker and bringing it up at the same time. The bandits kicked their mounts into high gear. One of the outlaws lagged behind and Presby saw

29

him twist in the saddle, cock his arm.

An object somersaulted through the air!

"Dynamite!" the deputy yelled.

The sheriff and deputy's horses split to either side as if by practised manoeuvre. They skidded into the brush at the trail's edge and the dynamite rolled along the ground where they had been. Their horses thrashed into the thicket, stumbling but keeping onward in an effort to put distance between them and the explosive.

A terrific blast shuddered the air and a hail of dirt and pebbles pelted their backs. The concussion slammed against them like an invisible fist, but they managed to hold their saddles and keep moving forward.

Presby shook off his shock and reined back on to the trail. Raising his Colt, he drew aim on the bandit who'd thrown the dynamite. The man had hung back to survey his handiwork. A mistake. A fatal one.

Presby's eyes narrowed and he steadied the Peacemaker. His finger eased the trigger in.

The outlaw yanked another stick of dynamite from his belt and fumbled for a lucifer.

Presby's gun blasted.

A rigidness slapped the bandit's body and the dynamite tumbled from his fingers. He sat stock still in the saddle and Presby took the panicked notion he'd missed.

The bandit pitched sideways and fell off his horse. The horse danced nervously, bolted.

"Got 'im!" the deputy shouted, raising a fist and shaking it.

Presby let out a long breath. They trotted up to the downed bandit, dismounting and bending over him. Presby pulled the mask away. "Recognize him?"

"Nope, no one I've seen before. You?"

"Can't say as I do."

The deputy cocked an eyebrow.

"There's one more. That one must have the jewels."

Presby nodded. "We'll leave this one. He ain't goin' nowhere."

They mounted and set their horses in motion after the second bandit. They rode hard, passing a log cabin that squatted a few paces from the stream, reaching a sprawling cemetery set deep to the side of the trail. Reining up, Presby shook his head.

"Where in tarnation could he have gotten to?"

The deputy shrugged. "Like the papers said, just vanished."

"No one just vanishes. He's here somewhere. Look, ain't no dust stirred up farther down the trail, no disturbed dirt. He stopped nearby and we're probably makin' ourselves a nice little target for him."

They exchanged looks and stepped from their saddles, guns drawn, alert for any sign of the second bandit. Presby surveyed the cemetery, the wooden crosses and thin headstones, the huge marble carving of an angel perched atop a huge square base. The angel seemed to peer down with a stricken expression and coldness settled into the pit of Presby's belly. The air was still, heavy, foreboding. Ghosts? The bandit had vanished somehow, though he knew it was impossible. But they weren't ghosts; his bullet had proved that. One outlaw was dead, but Presby wouldn't settle for half a job.

They spread out, each flanking the outskirts of the bone orchard, alert for movement. A squirrel chattered, making Presby jolt and spin. He gripped his nerves and moved forward, stopping as he heard a noise rise above the thrumming of his pulse in his ears — the snort of a horse. He spotted the animal, reins thrown loosely over an iron fence rail. He approached the bay, knowing it belonged to the bandit.

"Now, where — ?"

Another sound stopped him, one

he couldn't place the significance of: a thin grating. He had no time to dwell on it.

A shot jolted him. A leaden fist clubbed his belly. He knew the sound of guns, and that blast didn't belong to his deputy's Peacemaker.

He whirled, ran, heart pounding, for the spot he'd parted from his deputy. He slammed to a halt, jerking up his Peacemaker.

Two men stood before him; one, his deputy, a crimson rose blossoming across his shirt; the other, a hooded man holding a smoking Colt. The deputy's face washed with a blank expression and he crumpled to the ground.

Fury overtook Presby's shock. As the bandit whirled, Presby levelled his Peacemaker and fired. Lead jolted the outlaw before he could aim. He triggered a reflexive shot that gouged dirt from the ground, then collapsed.

Presby ran to him. The man was

breathing but would pose no threat. Presby grunted and, holstering his gun, went to the deputy. He lifted the man's head.

"Sorry . . . I let you . . . down . . . " the deputy said, words liquidy, weak. Blood trickled from his mouth.

"Hell, you didn't let no one down, son. We got the bastards! Got 'em dead clean. You'll be a hero. Just hang on and I'll get you to the doc." Presby saw the man force a weak smile, then his eyelids fluttered, closed.

A sick feeling swelled in Presby's soul. He had worked with the young man for a year now, had come to think of him as kin. He was a damn fine lawman and didn't deserve to die this way. He dreaded telling the man's family and doubted the glory of bringing down the Black Hood Bandits would make the task any less bitter.

Presby gently laid the deputy's head on the ground and straightened, glancing at the stones and marble angel. A hush

35

fell over the bone orchard, chilling him. He shook his head, then bent over the bandit and pulled off the hood. A surprised look turned his face and he muttered, "Sonofabitch!"

2

THE stage clattered into Hags Bend a shade past noon. It jounced and groaned, bucked and rattled, springs creaking and iron tires clanking with every bump and rut. It rolled to a halt in front of Hags Bend's only hostelry, carriage bobbing for a few seconds after the vehicle had stopped. The door popped open and a suited man stepped out, rolling his shoulders and drawing a deep breath to loosen the tenseness on his none-too-meaty frame. He eyed the driver, who looked down with an irritated bent to his features.

"Problem, gent?" the driver asked, tone sarcastic.

"Good God, man, when's the last time you had new springs installed on this, this, *thing*? I haven't had any feeling in my posterior since we left Cheyenne!"

The driver grunted, straightening and untying the sole piece of luggage atop the stage. He let a sideways grin slip on to his face and tossed the luggage to the street.

"Sit on that an' see if'n it don't make you more comfortable." He turned and squatted back into his seat, lashed the reins. The stage rattled into motion, stirring a cloud of dust that settled a fine film on the man's suitcoat.

Quinton Hilcrest jammed both fists into his hips and stared after the stage, muttering. "Well, this must be what they mean by western hospitality." His young features twisted into a tight frown and he sighed, glancing about the street. Hags Bend was a semi circular affair, small compared to any of the New England towns he'd seen, even his own of Portland, Maine. He spotted a general store, livery stable, sheriff's office, law office and dress shop, not much else. The wide main street sported ruts from wagon wheels and gouges from horse hooves. Only a few people moved along the boardwalk. That should make his job easier, but he had a feeling the creature comforts he was used to in the East would be hard found here. Maybe he should rethink his notion about settling out West with the reward money sure to be his when he found the jewels.

Maybe he shouldn't.

What was there for him back East anyway? His detective business? That was a laugh. Two customers in the last six months did not an enterprise make, and he was damn near out of money. He was staking all he had left on this trip West to chase 'some windmill' as Dora, his ex-fiancée, would put it. Some detective he'd turned out to be. He shook his head. So good he'd never suspected she was taking up with that, that, *man* until he'd caught her with the bloke quite by accident when he had closed up the office early one day — check that, when the bank had so graciously closed the office for him because he hadn't paid the rent in three months. Now all he owned resided in that suitcase coated with dust at his feet. That and the threadbare suit and worn derby perched atop his head, along with the derringer tucked in his inside coat pocket. Oh, he had a little cash left, money he had saved for the rent — he'd intended to pay it but, after all, a detective needed working capital — but that he would need for the necessities of western living and *other* things. It took bribery to work people's tongues loose oft'times and palm greasing was something he counted on doing in order to find the missing jewels.

Well, the East was behind him, now; so was Dora, God love her. He had travelled across lots to find his fortune and if that were going to happen he needed to start quick out of the gate. What cash he had would only last so long and he figured there would not be a whole lot of call for a detective in this neck of the woods.

He tugged loose the watch hanging

from a chain from his vest pocket, tapped it out of habit — sometimes it worked, sometimes it didn't — and saw the hands edge to half past noon.

He heaved up his suitcase, brushing it off best he could, then tried to put on a dignified air as he stepped across the boardwalk into the hotel. The hotel interior was simply decorated, with worn furniture and a dusty glass chandelier, but homey compared to the stuffy hotels of the East. He walked up to the desk and a craggy-faced clerk peered up at him from beneath a visor.

"He'p ya, gent?"

"Yes, my fine sir, I would like a room, one with a bath, please."

The clerk eyed him. "A bath?"

"Yes, I have been travelling and would like to soak."

"I can have one brought up fer ya for a little extra."

Quinton cocked an eyebrow. "Brought up? You mean to tell me there's no running water?"

41

The clerk scoffed. "Not 'less it grew legs."

Quinton sighed. "I suppose a telephone would be out of the question, then?"

"A what?"

"A telephone. You speak into one end and a voice comes out of the other."

The clerk's face twisted. "Ah, one of them newfangled things I heared about. Nope, ain't got one. The Devil's work, if'n you ask me. Got a telegraph over to Casper Ridge, south of here, though. You try there. Better than spook voices comin' out of a box."

"I see." Quinton gave another sigh and brought out a roll of bills, all he had left to his name. "A week should do for now. I'll let you know if it gets to be longer."

The clerk turned the register around and slid a pen towards Quinton. Quinton peeled off a bill and signed the book.

"First room to the right, up the

stairs," the clerk said, passing him a key. "Anything else you need, you just ask me and I'll do my best to git it — long as it don't involve no devil voices."

Quinton nodded, mouth crooked. He picked up his suitcase and walked to the stairs, turning back as a thought crossed his mind. "Where can I rent a motorbike?"

The clerk scrunched his face. "A what?"

Quinton nodded in resignation. "Never mind." He went up the stairs and located his room.

The room was small but held a comfortable bed and a semi-pleasant odor. He thought it smelled vaguely of perfume. A wash basin and pitcher sat on a bureau, mirror secured to the wall above it. Going to the basin he splashed lukewarm water onto his face and toweled off. He peered at his reflection in the mirror. He was a young man, handsome in a pretty-boy sort of manner, least compared with the rugged looks of men out here. His face was devoid of that weather-scoured look the locals sported, but he figured that would change after he made his fortune and started a new life in the West. He felt a little piqued he'd have to forego the luxuries of running water and telephones, but he supposed he could get used to it. Not that he had a whole lot of choice. Returning home meant facing bad memories and disappointments. For once in his life he was determined to make something of himself, grab the bull by the horns, so to speak. And Hags Bend was just the place to do it.

He pushed himself away from the bureau and lifted his suitcase on to the bed, opening it. Unpacking the few clothes and possessions he owned, he stuffed them into the bureau drawers. Lastly he took out the battered dime novel and surveyed the cover. The book, *The Black Hood Bandits Ride Again* was the reason he had come here. A sensationalist piece of writing, he admitted, but one he hoped, prayed, staked his wellbeing on, carried a germ of truth. He tucked the book into his pocket and closed the case, setting it on the floor at the foot of the bed.

If he were going to find those jewels, he'd best get a move on, hadn't he? He had mapped out his plan of attack on the uncomfortable stage ride from Cheyenne. In a town as small and isolated as Hags Bend, he saw limited possibilities. He would try the sheriff first; according to reports, he was the man responsible for bringing down the Black Hood Bandits. If the lawman proved uncooperative or unknowledgeable, he'd put Plan B into effect.

Quinton checked his watch and set out for the sheriff's office.

He strode along the boardwalk, eyeing the buildings and watching the fall breeze whisk dust sprites up in the street. The day was still warm, a muted heat that would soon trickle away as the season wound down and winter pummeled the land with cold and snow. That was something he had plenty of experience of in the East, though he had never cared particularly for the winter season. He'd care even less for it this year, when the tidings would only serve to remind him of what he'd lost — or perhaps had never had in the first place.

Unless he found those jewels . . .

He studied the signs before him, the Weeping Willow Saloon, Wentworth Law Office and Sheriff's farther on. He crossed the street and stepped up to the door.

A man with piercing grey eyes and a jaw as wide as a house peered up at him from behind a desk. A deputy sitting in a chair by a rickety table, looked up as well. Quinton considered himself to be a reasonable judge of people; he had to be in his profession. From the sheriff he got the immediate impression of a tough but fair man, one probably a step above some of the gunfighter-lawmen he'd heard about. The man boasted a reputation, in fact, one the dime novel blew out of proportion, but one that was deserved. He had brought down the Black Hoods, the ghost bandits who vanished into thin air.

The deputy, well, he was a different story. Something about him . . . Quinton couldn't put his finger on it, but while the fellow appeared clean cut there was a 'scent' about him, the invisible scent detectives learned to sniff out when they sized people up, clients or otherwise. The scent could stink, smell sweet as a rose or be just plain clean of odor. He was getting a whiff of weasel.

"What can I do for you, mister?" the sheriff asked when Quinton didn't speak immediately.

"Name's Quinton Hilcrest, Sheriff. I'm a detective from back East. I was hoping you might point me in some directions."

"Trail out of town's that way," said the deputy nudging his head towards the door. Quinton's 'scent' jumped

47

another notch on the stink meter.

"Now, now, Jenson," the sheriff said. "Give this fellow a chance. He might not be what we think he is."

Quinton's eyes narrowed. He considered not asking his next question but figured he'd get nowhere if he didn't. He pulled out the dime novel and held it out before the sheriff, who seemed to deflate.

"Galldamn, I'm sick to lily hell of you fellas comin' here!" He cast Quinton a disgusted look.

"Us fellas?" Quinton pocketed the book. The deputy chuckled, shook his head.

"Yep, you fellas. Let me take a wild guess: you read that there piece of garbage and figured it'd be right nice to find those jewels and collect the nice fat reward that goes with it."

"That's right." Surprise hung in Quinton's tone. "How'd you know?"

"How'd I know? Well, just that since that damn thing came out I musta

48

had a hunnert folks come in bent on doin' the same thing. All went away empty-handed and all were a big pain in the backside. Lucky they didn't get themselves killed."

Indignation bristled Quinton. "I'm different, Sheriff. I'm going to find those jewels." Quinton hadn't stopped to consider others might have read the book and hit on the same notion, but it made perfect sense. His hopes were buoyed by one piece of information, though: no one had yet found the jewels.

"So did they, mister — watcha say your name was?"

"Hilcrest, Quinton Hilcrest."

"Like I said, Mr Hilcrest, so did they. Fact of the matter is, them jewels are gone. Where, I don't rightly know, but it ain't damn likely anyone'll ever see hide nor hair of them again."

"Well, I'm out to prove you wrong, Sheriff. Hope you don't mind."

"Would it stop you if I did?"

"No."

49

The sheriff shrugged. "That all you came here for?"

"I was hoping you could steer me in the right direction."

"How you figure that?"

"Well, you did bring down the bandits, did you not?"

"Yeah, I did and I've been payin' for it ever since. You know how many ya-hoos with a chip on their shoulder decide they got the mettle to test a famous lawman?" Quinton shook his head. "Never thought about it."

"Well, too damn many, I'm here to tell you. Just as soon I'da let that gang escape that day. Woulda saved me a bellyful of grief."

"Ah, but the glory . . . " Quinton fought to keep the sarcasm out of his tone.

"Glory, hell! You know what glory means to two little girls and a mama who got me in their parlor tellin' 'em their daddy and husband ain't never comin' home 'cause he got killed for the glory?" Quinton shook his head, feeling guilty. "I'll tell you what it means, mister. It means spit. Ain't nothin' that can take the sting out of that kinda news, whether you just saved a hunnert innocent lives or returned a million in stolen jewels."

Quinton nodded slowly. The sheriff was right; nothing could take the sting out of that. He knew first hand what it felt like to lose someone you loved, though not in the same way. He made a mental note to check his cavalier attitude from now on.

"Still, I'd appreciate anything you could tell me that might be of help, Sheriff. I want those jewels returned — "

"And the reward in your pocket," Presby finished.

"Yes, that as well. I've staked everything I own on it, so don't think I've got no other reason than simple glory myself. I'll make sure a portion of that reward goes to that deputy's family when I find the jewels."

"Awfully sure of yourself, ain't ya?"

Quinton said yes, though deep down he felt unsure as hell. Why should this work out? Nothing else in his life had.

"Well, Mr Hilcrest, if your promise is good I'll tell you what I know, but I warn you it ain't much."

"You can count on it, Sheriff."

"You'd better see to it I can — not that I have a lick of confidence you'll find them, mind you, just that, well, that deputy of mine, he died a hero and his family deserves more than a wooden cross with a name burnt on it. Catch my meanin'?"

"Clearly. I'm a man of my word, Sheriff."

The sheriff nodded, a glint of doubt registering in his eyes. "All I know is the Black Hood Bandits robbed an inbound stage carrying a million worth of jewels. They got the stones, killed all the guards 'cept one. When I went after the fellas, one stopped and tried to show me Heaven's gates with a stick of dynamite. I got him first.

The other my deputy and I tracked to a cemetery a few miles north of here. Seemed he had just vanished. I found his horse tethered to a rail then I heard a shot. By the time I reached my deputy, the hardcase had shot him and I returned the favor. Unfortunately he lived so we had to waste time with a hangin'. The jewels weren't on him and after a search they didn't turn up."

Quinton's brow furrowed. "Well, that's it: he had to have stashed the jewels in the cemetery somewhere. He didn't have time to do anything else."

"Yeah. If it were that simple don't you think they'da been found by now?"

Quinton supposed the sheriff was right. A piece was still missing, one he had to find.

"I see what you're thinkin', Hilcrest, and don't. I won't stand for no grave-diggin'! 'Sides, he didn't have time to bury them."

Before Quinton could answer, the deputy leaned forward and said, "Why don't you just hightail it back where you came from fella? We chased enough tenderfoots outa here. Save us the trouble of doin' it again." The deputy drilled Quinton, a glint of — what? anger? hate? in his eyes. Quinton wasn't sure, but something told him the deputy wanted him on the next stage out of town for more reason than being another in a line of treasure hunters.

"I take it you don't want me looking into this, Deputy?" He put it bluntly, hoping to jolt the man, make him slip with something. The sheriff's gaze snapped to the deputy, a shade of suspicion suddenly in them. The deputy's gaze flicked from sheriff to Quinton and his face tightened.

"Jest we don't need no stirrin' up of the past here, Hilcrest." The deputy's tone had softened but Quinton heard a hollow ring to it.

"I plan on stirring up nothing but jewels, sir." Quinton tipped his derby and turned to walk out. He halted, glancing back at the sheriff. "I meant

54

what I said about the man's family, Sheriff. I have my decency."

"Just stay out of trouble, Hilcrest. Got plenty of room in my jail for them that don't."

On the boardwalk, Quinton paused. He had a slim lead, the cemetery, but if everyone had already looked for the jewels there and failed to find them . . .

Still, where else could they have gone? Could the bandit have stashed them somewhere along the trail? Would he have had time? The area, best he could judge from the ride in, covered a few miles of trail; it would be like searching for the proverbial needle in the haystack. That did little to encourage his hopes.

And what about the deputy? What about the man gave him a feeling of unease, a 'scent' of wrongness? He couldn't pinpoint it, but the man would bear watching.

Quinton started walking. He had learned little from the sheriff and in his mind it was time to try his second option.

He stopped beneath a wooden sign hanging above a door and peered up. The Weeping Willow Saloon. In the East, bars and pubs were usually a hotbed of gossip and tidbits of information. He figured the West would prove no different. Wherever people liked to drink tongues wagged.

Quinton opened the heavy wooden door and the reek of Durham smoke filled his nostrils. With it mixed the sour stench of old whiskey and stale perfume — the same vague scent he had sniffed in his hotel room. Glancing about he spotted a bargirl serving drinks and he put together what linked the two places. He'd heard stories about the gals of questionable reputations inhabiting drinkeries such as this. They had whores back East, just with different trimmings. Soiled doves, the dime novel had called them; that made as fine a tag as any. Women eager to separate a man from his earnings in whatever fashion it required. A thin smile touched his lips at that. Perhaps another source of information?

His eyes narrowed as he gazed through the haze clouding the room. A long polished bar ran the length of one wall and a silent piano rested against another. A smallish barkeep was setting bottles in a hutch behind the bar, next to which hung a gilt-edged mirror. A few tables held customers, most drinking and talking in too-loud liquored voices. At a green-felted table two men were playing some sort of game with dice — chuck-a-luck, if he recalled right.

"Just like the book says . . . " he mumbled, patting the dime novel tucked in his pocket. He felt strangely warmed by the scene, as if he'd just stepped into some other world he'd only fantasized about. Then he coughed as smoke choked his lungs and revised his assessment: it was a world that would take some getting used to, not a fantasy, but gritty and deadly, fashioned by men of steel muscle and iron will.

He threaded his way between the tables to the bar, planting himself on a stool. Setting his derby on the counter he ordered whiskey as the 'keep eyed him.

"Sure you can handle it, gent?" the 'keep asked in a voice that seemed way too deep for his small statue.

"You bet," Quinton answered with a high dose of cheer in his voice. He slid a silver dollar across the counter. The barkeep shrugged, grinned, plucked up the coin and poured the drink. Quinton lifted the glass in a toast and took a swig.

The whiskey came out in a spray. He did his best to swallow the amber liquid but coughed a stream across the counter. The 'keep bellowed a laugh and walked off. Quinton, red-faced, mopped his mouth on a coat-sleeve. He couldn't recall ever having tasted anything as vile. Damn close to petrol, it was. He cast the glass a wary look and tried another sip. The liquor seared his throat but he got it down, figuring he'd discover one aspect of western life he'd never get used to — make that *cotton to*, if he recalled the vernacular correctly: rot gut!

* * *

"Who's the tenderfoot who cain't handle his redeye?" asked one of the two men at the green-felted table. The other, a grizzled man with a flat nose and a perpetually crooked expression, shook the dice in his hand and rolled. "Jehosaphat! Snake eyes!" He ran a hand through hair as stiff as a wire brush. He twisted in his seat and eyed the suited man at the bar. "Easterner, name of Quinton Hilcrest. Here to find the jewels of the Black Hoods, like all them others."

The other gambler cast him a skeptical look. "How in tarnation you know that, Chuck-a-luck?"

"Other than treasure-seekers, how many damn tourists we get in Hags

Bend?" The other shrugged. "Not many. 'Sides, I shared a whiskey with the stage driver a spell ago."

The other fellow looked relieved. "Phew, thought yous mighta been spelled by that witch or somethin'."

"Witch, pshaw!"

"You wouldn't be sayin' that if'n you saw them evil dolls she makes. Devil's work, I tell ya!"

"Devil, hell! If there was a devil he sure as spit wouldn't come here. Nothin' in this neck of the woods for him to do. You're startin' to sound as superstitious as that lunk-headed hotel 'keep!"

"Well, I knows what I know. What he come for?" The man nudged his head towards Quinton.

"Told ya, the jewels. Comes from some place called Maine. Cold as hell, I hear."

"Ain't that the place where they eat them big red bugs?" The other's brow furrowed, nearly obscuring his eyes.

"Lobsters, they call 'em."

"Hell, a bug's a bug in my book. Looks like a big ol' scorpion and probably tastes like one."

Chuck-a-luck frowned. "Well, he's barkin' up the wrong tree if he thinks he'll ever find those jewels."

"Think so?"

"Look how many's tried and come up empty. 'Sides, once Deenie gets her claws in him he won't have no money left to go searchin' with!"

"Maybe you should be neighborly and warn him."

The bristle-haired man shrugged. "Some things a fella's just got to learn on his own and he looks the type who's about to get some schoolin' . . ."

3

"**B**UY a gal a drink, stranger?" The bargirl slid up beside Quinton and winked, flashing a veneer smile with too-red lips. Her dark eyes, shaded with kohl, carried a worn look, muddied by years in a business that caught up young women and discarded them by the time they reached their late twenties. Her cheeks, daubed with coral, were hollow and her hair was piled in fluffy curls. A blue sateen bodice heaved up her bosom. She reminded him of a kewpie doll, attractive in a garish forbidden sense. She wasn't like the eastern harlots he'd seen, that was for sure, and her manner warned of a conniving craftiness.

Quinton cocked an eyebrow at the girl, who batted long lashes and slipped a hand over his shoulder. "If it comes with some information," he said at last, suddenly feeling a little intimidated by the dove. He had read about these women, and even planned on targeting one for information, but being face to face with a woman straight out of a dime novel, well, that was another matter. Fact was, he had never had much luck or confidence with the ladies. His fiancée practically asked *him* for the engagement and after that he'd figured he was riding high. But everybody in Portland knew how *that* had turned out.

"Why, Deenie's just a well of information, honeybun. 'Specially when a handsome gent like yourself buys her pretty things and oils her brain with redeye."

He signalled the barkeep, who nodded, a funny expression turning his face. The 'keep brought a bottle and set it in front of Quinton, eyeing him and shaking his head.

"Fella, if you cain't handle redeye you cain't handle Deenie!" The 'keep walked off, chuckling.

Quinton looked back to the girl and she greased her crimson lips with a wooden smile and giggled an equally wooden giggle. "Oh, Charlie's just such a kidder. Don't you worry none, Deenie'll take right good care of a handsome gent like you."

Quinton tried a grin that didn't work, feeling uneasier by the moment. "I had a feeling you might."

"Ain't used to complaints, sugar."

Quinton decided to be direct. "I'm looking for information on the Black Hood Bandits. I intend to find the jewels they left behind."

She uttered a throaty laugh, pouring herself a drink and thumping the bottle on to the counter. "Well, honeybun, it'll take more than a little whiskey for help there!" She leaned in and he smelled the reek of too much perfume and sour whiskey. "Why don't you an' me go some place private and talk about it . . . " She winked and he almost said yes before it dawned on him what she was up to.

64

"Sorry, I'm not interested in having my money lifted while you get me drunk." It came out before he could stop it and he instantly regretted the statement as a dark storm filtered across her eyes and her lips tightened. That should have warned him. But it didn't. The next thing he knew he heard a resounding *crack*! and his face started stinging. A stunned moment later he realized she had hauled off and slapped him full across the face. It also dawned on him in that instant what one of his problems with women was: he sometimes lacked tact in talking to the fair sex. He could have politely fabricated an excuse to turn her down instead of calling her a thief outright, but no, he had chosen to disengage his brain and let his mouth take up the slack. Now his possible source of information had dried up and — if he judged correctly from the evil glint in her eyes — a slap would prove the least of his worries.

She swigged the rest of her glass in

a gulp. "You best take care who you go 'round insultin' with that sorta talk, fella. I'm right respectable, I am! And don't you forget it!" She whirled and strode off. His hand drifted to his face as he watched her go. His cheek felt numb. He turned to see the barkeep grinning.

"Told ya she was stronger than the redeye, fella!" the 'keep said.

"Guess I'll pay more attention next time," Quinton mumbled, sliding his jaw back and forth to make sure it still worked.

"Oh-oh . . . " The 'keep's eyes lifted to a spot behind Quinton; a distressed look crossed his features.

"What's wrong, now?" A dejected note laced Quinton's tone.

"Not a good idea to go 'round insultin' Deenie, fella. You'd best be takin' your hide outa here, *now*. Deenie's got friends and I don't want my place mussed up."

A sinking sensation slugged Quinton's belly. He lifted off the stool and turned, intending to heed the 'keep's advice this time and head for the door.

Two men stopped him.

The first, a barrel-built fellow with a dirt-smeared face and a missing tooth, jammed a ham-sized hand into Quinton's chest, shoving him back on to the stool. The second fellow, a smaller man with a weasel build, folded his arms and surveyed Quinton with a disparaging look.

"Hear tell you insulted our friend," the weaselly man said. "Ain't that right, Bord?" He glanced at the bigger man, who nodded, a half-smirk pulling at his lips.

"Way I hear it, Ted. Can't let that just pass on by. We gotta uphold the reputation of Miss Deenie."

Quinton sighed, the sinking feeling growing stronger. He shot a glance at Deenie, who gave him a sarcastic wave and a smug wink.

He spread his hands. "Look, fellas, I may have overstepped my bounds and for that I apologize. No harm done?"

He put on his best smile and friendliest manner, saying a silent prayer.

"No," said the weaselly man, shaking his head. "No harm done at all, 'cept to Miss Deenie's honor."

Quinton knew a split second before the bigger man's fist sailed towards him he wouldn't be able to talk his way out of it. He also knew that one of the few things he had done right back East was about to earn its keep.

The fist slammed into the counter just below where Quinton's head had been. As soon as the burly man's arm went into motion Quinton had pitched sideways, ducking under the blow and off the chair. The weaselly man made a grab for him, getting fistfuls of his suitcoat. Quinton's arms knifed up and out, snapping the man's hold.

The weaselly assailant appeared vaguely puzzled about the move. Apparently he wasn't used to having his hold broken and it stopped him short. That gave Quinton a slim advantage.

Quinton let out a yell and anchored

one leg, whirling and letting fly with the other. The spinning sidekick slammed into the man's belly.

The fellow flew backwards, an *omph*! exploding from his lips. He hit the bar, the perplexed look on his face deepening to shock and pain. As he doubled, gasping and clutching his gut, Quinton sent a chopping blow to the back of his neck. The weaselly attacker straightened, pitched forward like an axed tree. A cloud of sawdust billowed as he slammed into the floor.

The barrel-built man clubbed a fist at the back of Quinton's head just as Quinton turned towards him. He saw the blow coming, jerked his head to avoid it but couldn't get out of the way in time. The blow glanced from his noggin, sent him stumbling, a curtain of variegated speckles glittering before his eyes.

His mind tumbled and the room snapped in and out of darkness. The next thing he knew he was sitting on his rump, staring up with a glazed look.

The burly man loomed over him and grabbed his suitcoat. Quinton felt himself heaved up into a standing position.

The attacker jammed his face close and sour breath assailed Quinton's nostrils, snapping him to awareness.

The burly man released one hand and cocked it for a hammering blow, intent on shortening Quinton's neck.

Quinton jerked his head sideways, jabbing two fingers into a soft spot just below the elbow of the arm holding him.

The barrel-built man bleated, let go, clubbing at the same time. The blow missed Quinton's head, grazed his shoulder. A welt of numbness and pain shot to the tips of his fingers.

Clutching his arm, the attacker narrowed his eyes in fury. He roared and charged, murder in his eyes.

Quinton sidestepped. As the man careened past, Quinton snatched an arm and, using the fellow's weight and momentum against him, whirled the man about, sending him forward like a loosed cannon ball. The attacker tried to correct his flight, but couldn't. He sailed over a table and through the front window. A jangle of glass, followed by the thud of a body slamming into the boardwalk, sounded. Then silence.

Quinton gasped a breath, chest heaving, heart hammering. He peered at the weaselly man, who crawled about on the floor, wiping a snake of blood from the corner of his mouth. Deenie stepped up to the fallen man and grunted, looking disgusted.

"Ain't you two just the sorriest kind!" She spat on the man. "Cain't even defend my honor against a little drink of water like that." She thumped a bootheel on the man's head and he collapsed, out cold.

Deenie cast Quinton, who was rubbing his shoulder, a corrosive look and stalked off. Around the bar-room, the few other customers gawked, first at the fallen man, then at Quinton, then at the window.

The saloon door rattled open and Quinton looked up to see Sheriff Presby stepping through, deputy in tow. The sheriff sighed and removed his hat as he walked toward Quinton after swinging his gaze about the room. Behind him the barrel-built man, red-faced, stumbled in, pointing.

"That's him, Sheriff. That's the one who done it!"

The sheriff shook his head and crinkled his brow, as if he couldn't quite put together how a man of Quinton's size and genteel looks could possibly have mopped the floor with two rowdies.

"You again!" Presby said. "Well, what you got to say for yourself?"

Quinton eyed the burly attacker, then the sheriff. "These men seem to think I insulted their friend. I apologized yet they refused to accept it."

"So you decided to beat them silly?" Disbelief weighted the sheriff's question.

"They attacked me. I had no choice but to defend myself."

"Well . . . " The sheriff scratched his head. "Bord says different. Says you waylaid 'im without cause. Imagine Ted will back that up whenever he sees fit to wake up." The sheriff's tone indicated he didn't believe the burly man. "I'd just as soon lock you all in the same cell for a night and see who comes out on top."

Quinton bristled. "That's ridiculous, Sheriff! These men clearly attacked me. I had every right to defend myself."

The sheriff blew a long sigh. "Look, you may think you got a handle on everything, Mister Easterner, but out here we got a different way of workin' things. I ain't about to take your word 'less you come up with some witnesses, 'cause it'll be two against one when he" — the sheriff nudged his head to the unconscious Ted — "wakes up and I'm right inclined to go with the majority."

Quinton's irritation strengthened. He

73

had been in Hags Bend a little over an hour and already things were heading the way they always did — straight down the chute.

"Look here, the 'keep saw the whole thing!" Quinton turned to the 'keep, who peered at them from behind the bar.

"Well?" Presby asked.

The 'keep shrugged. "He's right, Sheriff. These fellas tried to put some hurt on 'im. He did what he had a right to do."

The sheriff grunted. "That makes it two against two, Hilcrest. Reckon I can tell ya I'm more inclined to believe the word of the 'keep than anything these yahoos say." He drilled the barrel-built man, who twisted his lips into a sneer. "But still . . ."

"I'll vouch for 'im, Sheriff."

They turned to see the wire-haired gambler coming up to them. In one hand, he clacked a pair of dice and with the other he tipped an imaginary hat. "These hombres tried to make this

74

young fella here cold as a wagon tire."

"You shore 'bout that, Chuck-a-luck?" The sheriff's tone held disappointment, Quinton thought.

"Sure as I'm sittin' there losin' my britches in that game with Freddy." He jabbed a finger at the other gambler, who nodded.

"Well Hilcrest, they just pulled your fat out of the fire." The sheriff looked at Bord again, who appeared indignant.

"Hold on just a damn minute, Sheriff!" Bord gestured angrily at Quinton. "You can't take the word of this, this *pansy*!"

The sheriff chuckled. "This pansy just wiped the floor with you and your partner, Bord. I told ya I'd have no more out of either of you. I think you and Ted deserve a night compliments of Iron Bar Hotel. You got a problem with that?" The sheriff cast Bord a challenging look.

Bord clamped his mouth shut.

The sheriff nodded towards the fallen man and said to the deputy, "Haul him over to the jail. Let him sleep it off in there."

The deputy nodded, looking none too pleased, and gazed at Quinton. "Told ya to watch yourself, fella. Don't go steppin' too hard after this. You could fall through a hole." He whisked past Quinton, bumping him slightly, and bent over the fallen man. Hauling him up and over a shoulder, he lugged him from the saloon.

"You best take that advice, Hilcrest. I'll let it pass this time, but I won't cotton to any more trouble. Catch my meanin'?"

"Emphatically, Sheriff."

The sheriff herded Bord from the saloon. Quinton watched them leave then turned to the man who had corroborated his story.

"Name's — "

"Quinton Hilcrest," interrupted the man. "I know. Everybody knows everybody in Hags Bend."

"Then it appears you have me at a disadvantage, sir." He proffered his hand and the man took it.

"They call me Chuck-a-luck Jones, on account I like to do me a bit of gamblin'."

"Well, sir you took a gamble a moment ago standing up for me and I appreciate it. Least I can do is buy you some of that swill they pawn off as liquor here."

Chuck-a-luck grinned, the perpetually crooked tilt to his face strengthening. He jutted a thumb at the door. "Them fellas? Ain't much risk there. They're ninety percent harmless."

"It's the other ten percent that worried me. I do believe they intended extreme harm on my person."

"You got a funny way of talkin', Mr Hilcrest — "

"Quinton, please."

"Quinton, it is. But hell, they'da just worked you over a bit and left you alone. Sort of a ritual here. They think it'll get them Deenie's respect, but she always ignores them after they do her dirty work."

77

They took stools at the bar and Quinton signaled the barkeep to bring another bottle, the first having been broken when Ted slammed into the bar and knocked it to the floor.

"Say, what was that fancy stuff you were doin'? Some of that Oriental fightin' I heard tell about?"

"That, my friend, is called kung fu — the one thing I did right back East. Saved my backside a few times over, I'll tell you that."

Chuck-a-luck rubbed his flat nose. "Right falootin' stuff. That the reason you came here, other than the treasure, 'cause nothin' was goin' your way?"

"News does get around fast, doesn't it?"

"Old by the time you make it."

"Well, my friend, maybe it is the reason. Maybe I'm thinking about starting anew and this just might be the place."

Chuck-a-luck scoffed. "You could be in for another disappointment, son. Ain't nothin' in Hags Bend but a lack of progress and evil spirits if you ask the hotel clerk or my gamblin' pardner yonder."

"Evil spirits?" A puzzled look twisted Quinton's features.

"Ain't important. So you aim to find that Black Hood treasure?"

"Yes, I do. Have my plan all mapped out and I'll turn it up, you wait and see."

"Hate to tell you how many fellas has said such. You probably won't be the last neither. Hope you ain't stakin' too much on it."

Everything, Quinton almost said, but held back. If this didn't work out — well he didn't know what he'd do and thinking about it made his belly tumble.

"I'll find it. Already got a lead." He pulled out the dime novel and slapped it on the counter. "Near everything I need to know about how the bandits worked is in here."

Chuck-a-luck shook his head as he picked up the book. "You cain't go 'round believin' this stuff, Quinton. It's all just a bunch of words. Real life ain't like a book."

"There you are right, Chuck-a-luck. But there's a shred of truth behind every exaggeration and I intend to ferret it out."

"A fool's errand, you know that?" Chuck-a-luck ran a hand through his bristly hair. "But by damn I think you're dead serious."

"I *am* serious . . . " Quinton got a twinge in the pit of his stomach, telling him the man was right: he *was* on a fool's errand and he'd only end up disappointed and empty-handed again. But with one difference; this time he would have nowhere else to turn. The last of his money would be gone and he doubted he could survive out West using just his two hands. Beyond the kung fu, he had never been the rough-and-ready type.

"You know anything that would help?" he asked Chuck-a-luck.

"Hell, if I did, I'da found the damn

treasure myself by now! Reckon I'm commencin' to think those jewels never even existed or if they did they're missin' for good."

"Says in the book the lone living guard insists they were aboard the stage. So does the manifest that became public after the incident. And there's a party in California offering a big reward for their recovery."

Chuck-a-luck shrugged. "Me, I'll have to see 'em to believe 'em!"

"When I find them I'll show them to you, Chuck-a-luck! Then you'll have to believe."

"Even then I'll have my doubts." Chuck-a-luck smiled. "Thanks for the whiskey, Quinton. I'd best be gettin' back to my game. I got a losin' streak to uphold!" Chuck-a-luck pushed himself off the stool and Quinton did the same, perching his derby atop his head.

"Say, you don't know where I can find suitable transportation, do you?"

Chuck-a-luck smirked. "Try the livery stable down the street . . . "

Quinton had ridden a horse only once in his twenty-seven years, back East with Dora. She had informed him riding was a mark of proper breeding. He had picked up the basics of English style, but never enjoyed it. Being atop the animals made his head spin and his rear complain.

Out West, however, he saw little choice. Hansom cabs and motorbikes proved non-existent.

From the saloon, he had walked to the livery stable and rented the beast beneath his legs now, a mule-hipped, whey-bellied bay that stood about fourteen hands. After having the attendant saddle the animal, Quinton had urged the bay along the street at a slow walk, getting the feel. The first few hundred feet proved rocky ones. With every jounce his teeth clacked and more than once he got the idea he would pitch out of the saddle. His tailbone already had a knot in it. The bay seemed to take it in stride, giving a snort occasionally, but little other sign of objection. Quinton was thankful the attendant had not set him up with an ill-tempered horse.

After the first tippy mile, he learned to ride with the animal, getting the feel of the horse's stride and rhythm. A long throw from feeling at ease, but better than aggravating his sore bottom.

He trotted along the hard-packed trail, eyeing the woodland ablaze with the colors of October. The sweet-sour scent of decaying leaves perfumed the air, which had turned almost brisk as the day wore on. To either side, oaks, pines, fir, birch and maples rose to touch the heavens. In the distance he spotted the gun-metal-colored peaks of the Rockies stabbing puffy cotton clouds. A feeling of peace wandered over him for the first time since he had come to Hags Bend. The serenity of the woodland, the fragrance of the season made him feel almost secure, at home. There was far less commotion here than in the hustle-bustle cities of the East. The tranquillity embedded itself in your soul, made you feel a part of all living things. He heard the chattering of the squirrels, their scurrying through the brush, and saw a bald eagle sail across the robin's egg-blue sky. The brassy sun gleamed from the fall leaves, igniting an inferno of brilliant color — red, orange, gold. He drew a deep breath, letting it out slowly, tension draining from his muscles. He could get used to this, by God he could.

If only he could find those jewels.

The jewels. Where could they be? He studied the ground as he rode, spotting no signs of where the stage had overturned, evidence scoured away by rain and wind and iron tires. If the bandit had stashed the jewels in the woods or somewhere along the way, they might never be found. That might explain why no one had.

Yet Quinton coddled the feeling, whether from false hope or blind faith, the bandit wouldn't have done that. In his mind, he saw the bandit stashing them wherever they stashed themselves when they pulled their disappearing acts. That was the only thing that made sense to him — or at least the only thing he would accept as making sense.

The cemetery? If the jewels were there, why hadn't they been found by now? Treasure-hunters had scoured the area and come up empty-handed.

Empty-handed. Was that what Quinton was destined for as well?

"You have to get off this train, Quinton, my boy," he scolded himself. "This time you have to come through!"

He hoped he could convince himself of that and alleviate the gnawing feeling he was chasing another windmill.

A woman stepped on to the trail a hundred feet ahead of him, taking him from his thoughts. He slowed the horse. "What the — " he muttered, straightening in the saddle, suddenly remembering his last encounter with a woman in Hags Bend. He'd decided to swear them off, but there appeared no way to go around her.

She was dressed in a simple blouse and skirt that hugged her curves. Chestnut hair fell in gentle cascades over her shoulders.

A log cabin came into view near a stream that meandered through a clearing. He guessed that was where the woman was headed.

As he drew closer, he noticed she carried something: dead flowers, he determined on closer inspection. He sat his horse and the woman, he placed her age at about twenty-five, glanced up at him, expressionless. A tingle coursed through him as she looked at him with the loveliest blue-green eyes he had ever seen. Her face was lovely as well, though it showed signs of hardship and a ghost of — what? Sorrow, maybe. Sadness.

"You gonna say somethin' or just keep on starin' at me?" she asked, breaking his spell. He noted her tone held a challenge, though he couldn't guess for what reason.

"Sorry, miss, just that you're a lovely sight for sure." Aw, damn, he scolded himself, forgetting to temper his usual bluntness again. He hoped this woman didn't have two bodyguards waiting in the cabin.

The woman scoffed and frowned. "If I didn't know better, I might take that as a compliment."

"I'd be honored if you did."

The frown grew deeper. "You must be new in town . . . "

"Just arrived this afternoon. I came to find the Black Hood jewels. Know anything that could help?"

"You don't waste much time with the amenities, do you, stranger?"

"Sometimes that gets me in trouble, but I haven't hit on a better way, yet."

"You're takin' your chances talkin' to me, you know that, don't you?"

"Seems like I'm taking my chances talking to any woman in this neck of the woods."

She gave him a perplexed look, but didn't comment. "Haven't you heard the talk?"

"Talk?" It was his turn to look puzzled.

"Well, mister, why don't you just come back after you do. See if you still think I'm so 'lovely', then." She spun and hurried off, her words holding a somber, almost damning note. Though he sensed a sorrow about her again, he couldn't begin to fathom what she had meant. One thing he could fathom: a woman like that could be a whole lot of trouble for a ne'er-do-well like him and he'd best vanquish the notion taking shape in his mind.

He shook his head and gigged his bay onward, riding about half a mile before stopping in front of the cemetery the sheriff had told him about. A rusty iron fence that reached to his shoulders surrounded the bone orchard. The gate dangled from one hinge. Dead leaves blanketed the cemetery proper, which showed signs of disrepair.

Dismounting, legs shaky and sore, he walked through the gate. Beneath his shoes, leaves felt like a spongy cushion, slick in places from a recent rain. A hush weighed on the surroundings, broken by the whisper of brittle leaves, like spook voices. He fought the urge to shiver. Surveying the stones and wooden cross markers, he noted nothing out of the ordinary — and nothing that might lead him to the jewels. Coming to a huge marble angel, perched atop a base that rose well above his head, he stopped. The angel seemed to gaze down on him with a disdainful expression, telling him he had wasted his time coming here, that he'd never find the jewels. The notion played on his mind, discouraging him. How could he hope to find them where so many had failed? It *was* a waste of time and he would have to pay the consequences.

No! He couldn't give up yet! He had given up too many times before. He'd given up on the East and his detective agency and run to the middle of nowhere, all because he felt somehow out of place and useless after Dora. If that happened here, it would happen everywhere. Forever. This was his last chance to prove to himself he could set a goal and see it through. He couldn't give up.

Yet.

He moved around the angel, walking the perimeter of the bone orchard, discovering nothing to point him in the direction of the jewels. His resolve started to erode. Reaching the edge of the cemetery, he paused, eyeing a chipped weathered stone carved with a name, a boy's name. The dates indicated the boy had been only twelve when he died. At the base of the stone rested a bundle of fresh flowers and his mind jumped back to the woman on the trail. She had been carrying dead flowers. Had she put the fresh ones down? He guessed she had.

A question crossed his mind: was this the reason for the sorrow he'd sensed about the woman?

Why should that be of any interest to him? He had sworn off women, hadn't he?

He peered at the grave, a chilled sensation creeping along his spine. He had a powerful urge to go back to her and ask, but thought better of it when Deenie's face sprang to mind. The woman had said something about the talk in town. Perhaps he'd best find out what she meant before jumping into anything.

He hoped he would heed his own advice, but wouldn't have laid a bet on it.

Quinton gave the search another half-hour. He picked through the bone orchard leaf by leaf, poking into every nook and cranny, but coming up the same as the rest: with a handful of nothing.

Shuffling back to his horse, he mounted, easing his tender backside into the saddle. He needed more, some clue to point him towards the jewels. But where would he find that? At the moment he didn't even have a notion where to look.

"Some detective you are . . . " he chided himself. No wonder he never had any business back East.

4

AN idea struck Quinton on the ride back into town, and he felt pleased with himself for it. Hags Bend might be a backwoods speck on the map, but he recalled noticing a small newspaper office on his way out of town to the cemetery. That would prove as good a place as any to continue his search for clues.

He nudged his bay up to the shabby little affair of a building and parked — 'sat' was the word they used in these parts — *sat* his horse in front of the Hags Bend *Sampler*. Dismounting, forcing his cramped legs to straighten, he tethered the animal to the rail and stepped across the boardwalk. The door rattled and a bell above it clinked as he walked in.

The reek of fresh ink and pulp paper assailed his nostrils; he scrunched his nose closed. Glancing about, he saw slanted benches covered with page set-ups, desks, files against the walls and a rickety printing contraption at the back of the room. Behind the machine, feeding a sheet into the contraption and cranking a large handle, squatted the roundest specimen of a woman he'd laid eyes upon. She couldn't have topped 4' 7" but was damn near as wide. A blue visor arched over compressed moon features sporting a mouth wide as a Cheshire cat's. Her clothes, taut blouse that bulged in more locations than it should have and trousers hitched half-way over the mound of her belly, were rumpled, as if she'd lived in them for weeks. Curly grey-brown hair stuck out from beneath the visor at peculiar angles.

"Help ya, gent?" the woman asked, glancing up, at the same time waddling to the other end of the machine to pull out a printed sheet.

Quinton painted on his best smile and removed his derby. "Why, yes, my fine lady, I think you can. I was hoping you could provide me with some information on the Black Hood Bandits."

She cocked an eyebrow. "Why you interested?"

He noted she had a voice like a freight train. "Well, ma'am . . ." He decided to be straightforward. He got the impression she was no woman to put up with beating around the bush, but of course where women were concerned, well, he had made a few miscalculations. "I came to find the missing jewels and return them to their rightful owner."

"And collect yerself a nice fat reeward — don't ya try to buffalo me, Mr — ?"

"Hilcrest. Quinton Hilcrest."

"Mr Hilcrest. Better men have tried." She slapped her ink-blotched hands on her trousers and spat on the dusty floor. A very unfeminine gesture, Quinton noted with some disgust, though he kept the expression off his face. His gaze absently scanned the floor as he took a step forward.

"Ah, you've seen through me. I suspected a fine woman such as yourself wouldn't stand for any balderdash." He let his smile broaden and kept his voice as sincere as possible.

The fleshy woman beamed. "Well, you certainly have a nose for folks, then, don't ya, fella? You're right on the mark, awright — you some kind of lawman?"

"Right you are. A detective from the East come to close the case on the Black Hoods once and for all. My card — " He fished in a suitcoat pocket, bringing out a small card embossed with his name and defunct agency and handed it to her. She snatched it up with sausage-shaped fingers and studied it. He had an instant of worry she wouldn't believe him. She tucked the card into a grimy pocket and smiled a smile with two missing teeth.

"I like your style, gent. Right better than the hog-wallow upbringin' the fellas in these parts got themselves. What can I do ya for?"

"Well, miss — ah, I don't believe I caught your name."

"Malone. Molly Malone."

"Well, Miss Malone, I got to thinking, now who would be the most likely person to furnish the information I need, and lo and behold hit upon the idea of this fine establishment."

The woman beamed again. "Well, I do run a spic an span operation here, Mr Hilcrest. Any news fit to print, well, howdy, you'll find it in the *Sampler*. How perceptive of you to notice."

"Well, ma'am, I do try. I do try. But back to the Black Hoods for a moment."

"Aw, yessir. You come to the right place. Got me everything there is to know on the *hombres*. Kept a special file of all the articles I ever printed on 'em. They was right big news in these parts a spell back. Mostly I jest get me the regular stories 'bout pig stealin' and such, but them Black Hoods, they was front page for a piece." She spat on the floor again. "Hell, ever' once in a spell someone comes in thinkin' he can find the jewels — oh, not like yourself, of course, Mr Hilcrest. No siree. None of 'em's ever been smart enough to come here and ask and I didn't volunteer nothin', neither. But since you're so perceptive, I'll let you see my file."

He performed a half bow. "I'd be pleased, indeed, Miss Malone. Pleased, indeed."

She held up a porky finger. "Now, you just hold your britches and I'll find it." She waddled over to a file and rifled through the various folders, finally pulling out one marked with a tag that said The Black Hood Robberies, and a flask.

She handed him the file, which bulged, and held out the flask. "Care for a nip, Mr Hilcrest?" She eyed him and he had the sudden impression he'd better accept.

"Why, don't mind if I do, Miss Malone." He took the flask, swallowing

98

a mouthful and doing his best not to cough up the fiery liquor. It burned worse than the rotgut at the saloon.

His face pinched and he passed the bottle back to her. "Good stuff," he managed to croak.

She slapped him on the back; the blow rattled his bones and took him two steps forward. She brayed a laugh. "Like I always say, Mr Hilcrest, man who won't drink with me ain't got no sand. You got yourself some sand, Mr Hilcrest, shorely you do!"

"Appreciate the compliment." He hoped the sarcasm didn't show in his tone.

"Now, don't you fret none. You just take your fine self to that desk yonder and take your time. I'd right enjoy the company." She winked and he felt a heavy sensation in his belly he couldn't pin on the whiskey.

He went to the desk and lowered himself slowly into the chair. The chair creaked and tilted and he damn near fell over backwards. "Dash it all! The chairs in this town are as hard to ride as the horses," he blurted.

"What's that, Mr Hilcrest?" Molly asked, eyeing him.

"Ah, nothing. Just remarking on the completeness of this file." He patted the folder.

He opened the file and pored over the mound of clippings. Most were from other newspapers in the area, detailing the activities of the bandits in Wyoming. Most of their robberies took place within a fifty-mile range of Hags Bend. He had known that but the fact still surprised him that they could range such a small area and simply vanish. One thing stood out: Hags Bend was the focal point. That meant their hideout had to be nearby.

As he read, he began to have a growing if morbid respect for the bandits. With each crime they had become craftier, bolder, bloodier, striking at just the right place at just the right time — at least until the last couple

100

of hold-ups: a bank robbery in Casper Ridge, where they got away with only a pittance, and the jewel heist in Hags Bend, which had resulted in their downfall. He noted another point: each article seemed to dwell on the fact that the use of the dynamite by the bandits increased with each job. That had contributed to their ruin. When the bandit stopped to blow up the sheriff, the tables had turned. Had he kept riding chances were they would have pulled another disappearing act. A pattern, but one that offered him little help. Nothing gave an indication to the whereabouts of the jewels. The articles merely provided him with a curious respect for the robbers who had terrorized the area. It was the stuff of legend, the stuff of dime novels. He had seen reputations concocted on far less.

He sifted the articles together, scanning a last one that related the events of the surviving robber's hanging. The man had lived through the gunshot, though probably wouldn't have survived more than a few weeks because of its seriousness. The sheriff had not given him the chance. He had been sentenced the next morning without the benefit of a trial. The bandit had been escorted to a hastily erected gallows and hanged until the Black Hood Bandits passed into dime-novel fodder.

Quinton was about to slap the folder closed when a final point caught his eye. A name: Wentworth. The bandit's name was Calvin Wentworth.

His brow furrowed. Where had he heard . . . ?

Of course! The law office! The law office sign had carried the same name. Were they connected?

He slapped the folder shut and stood. Molly Malone eyed him with a look dogs gave steaks and shuffled up to him.

"Find anything useful, Mr Hilcrest?"

"Maybe, my dear Miss Malone. An article, one penned by yourself, I believe."

She grinned. "That'd be the necktie party. I was there. Watched him pass on to the road to hell, Mr Hilcrest. A sunny day t'was too. You should have seen the jig he did hangin' from that — "

"Ah, yes," he cut in, feeling his stomach turn. Hanging seemed on par with Saturday dances as far as entertainment went out West, but he had never found death particularly enthralling as a spectator sport. "The name of the bandit . . . ?"

"Wentworth, Calvin Wentworth. Funny thing is, everybody knew the scalawag. Always thought he was a bad one, but never did anything you could pin on him. Hell, you see, I got me this side job selling some fancy painted mussel shells I get from a fella in San Francisco. Throw 'em in a wheel barrow once a month and go 'bout town. Wentworth always bought some and was always cordial."

"All the time he was right in your midst?"

She nodded, chins jiggling. "Reckon that's how they vanished so well. The other *hombre* nobody saw before, but I figure he must have come from one of the surrounding towns."

"I saw a law office on the way into town by the same name. Any relation, by chance?"

"Why, yes, that's Norvell Wentworth. A distant cousin, if I recollect. Moved in 'bout a month after they stretched ol' Cal's neck."

"I see." A light blinked on in Quinton's mind and the woman seemed to pick up on it.

"Now, don't you go gettin' any funny ideas. Mr Wentworth's nothing like his cousin. A right respectable man, he is." Quinton had the sudden impression the lawyer had spent some time charming Molly — "Used to come in here and bring me news fit to print, even shared a swig of whiskey, so I know he's upstandin'."

Quinton nodded, debating her method for measuring a man's trustworthiness.

"Anybody else make the connection?"

"At first folks treated him with a wary eye, but I took to him right off. They came 'round after he set up his business. Did some folks some free work, gained their confidence and respect. He showed 'em he wasn't like his cousin. Hell, he's even got a relative workin' for the sheriff, so that proves he's awright."

"The deputy?" Surprise struck Quinton's face. "The deputy is related to Wentworth?"

"Yep, 'nother cousin, I believe. Not quite as upstandin' as Norvell, if you ask me."

"Why's that?" Quinton neglected to tell her the impression of the deputy he'd garnered.

"Well, jest that there's rumors he's been takin' up with that Deenie over to the Willow. You know, that hussy's gonna lead that boy to no good if somethin' ain't done. She's a conniving little — "

"Ah, yes, I've had the pleasure,"

Quinton cut in. "Not the type of gal I'd be asking to a cotillion, I assure you."

"Hell, you need a dancin' partner, Mr Hilcrest, you come to me. I'm right light on my feet."

Probably not on mine, he thought, keeping the expression from his face. "I'm sure you are, Miss Malone. I'm sure you are." He passed the folder back to her. "I thank you for your help, kind lady."

"You find them jewels, Mr Hilcrest, I 'xpect you owe me a bottle and the scoop." She held up the flask.

He accepted it begrudgingly and swallowed a gulp, his insides lighting up. "I'm a man of my word . . ."

★ ★ ★

The clippings had told him little but they had pointed him down another road in his pursuit of the jewels. Molly Malone might take a man's word based on the fact he drank with her,

106

but Quinton wasn't that trusting. He intended to pay Mr Norvell Wentworth a visit and judge for himself. Though he hadn't met the man, something about the lawyer already bothered him. That 'scent' he relied on so much had begun to stink like skunk on a dog — ah, there! a westernism, as they called it back home. Perhaps he was getting used to this town after all.

Angling a smile, he led his horse along the street, reluctant to climb into the saddle again. He felt blisters where he sat and swore he was no longer walking as straight as when he came into Hags Bend.

The more he thought it over, the more something else piqued his curiosity and his suspicion about Wentworth. The lawyer was related to the deputy, a deputy who had given Quinton every impression of a man who would just as soon let the whole Black Hood business fade into obscurity and scare off anyone who took an interest. That smacked of entirely too big a coincidence. He had stumbled across bigger ones that didn't pan out, but his gut feeling told him there was something there. He intended to find out. He stopped in front of the lawyer's office, surveying the gilt letters etched on to the large window and sign above the door. Lawyers . . . the man who'd taken his fiancée had been a lawyer. Maybe it contributed to his reluctance to give Norvell Wentworth the benefit of the doubt. Petty, true, but he couldn't shake it. He also couldn't let it cloud his rationale.

He hitched his bay to the rail and walked up to the door, opening it.

A man with a jowly face and onyx eyes looked at him from behind a large desk. The 'scent' started stinking immediately. The man gave Quinton the impression of a squirrel who had just hoarded all the nuts. His mind momentarily flashed back to the day he had caught Dora — "

Remember what you told yourself about not clouding your rationale! he scolded himself. Although first impressions usually proved right for him, he needed more than a squirrelly look to convict a man.

He scanned the office, removing his derby and fidgeting with the brim. The desk, some dark wood he couldn't place, held a high polish. He spotted a painting, French, he guessed, and expensive, on one wall. A portrait of President Grover Cleveland hung on another. A copy of *The Adventures of Huckleberry Finn*, Twain's latest, lay on a table sporting cabriole legs and ball-and-claw feet. A rich carpet adorned the center of the room. The whole appearance crafted a look of elegance and expense. Quinton had the idea it was like gold coating on a hollow Easter egg.

"What can I do for you, sir?" Norvell Wentworth asked, rising and extending a hand. Quinton stepped up and took the hand, noting the man's grip was strong enough to crack a walnut. The lawyer towered a good six inches above him, outweighed him by maybe seventy-five pounds. An intimidating presence. He could see how a man like this might charm Molly Malone, but around others he appeared the type to merely bowl over anyone not inclined to his opinion.

Quinton debated the best approach to use on the man, surprising himself that he gave it any consideration at all. Maybe he had learned something from his experience with Deenie.

Maybe not.

He decided in this case the blunt approach was the one to use again. He certainly couldn't sweet talk a man like Norvell Wentworth the way he had Molly and he couldn't buffalo or frighten him, either.

"Well, Mr Wentworth, I hope you can do something for me."

Norvell Wentworth lowered himself into his seat and indicated a chair in front of the desk. Quinton winced and sat, the padding thick as a cloud to his relief.

"Fire away, sir. Is it a legal matter?

I'm your man, then. What is it — land swindle? Woman done you wrong?"

"One out of two, Mr Wentworth, but that isn't why I came here."

"No?" Wentworth's jowly face showed vague interest. He opened a humidor on his desk and selected a cigar, jamming it between his lips. "Offer you one, sir?" He struck a match, puffing the stogy's end to glowing red.

"I'll pass. Hay fever, you know."

"Of course. You Easterners always were a bit on the unhealthy side."

Surprise glinted in Quinton's eyes. "How'd you know I was from the East?"

"News gets around in such a small town, sir. I would have known it from the way you are dressed, if it weren't for the fact that I already heard all about you. Your name is Quinton Hilcrest and you're a detective from Maine."

Quinton got the idea he'd been talking to his relative, the deputy. "Then you know why I'm here?"

The expression on Wentworth's face darkened. Wentworth was not a man particularly adept at hiding his emotions. Men used to getting their way through intimidation usually weren't. "The Black Hood jewels . . . "

"Right to the point, Mr Wentworth, that's the way I like it. In that case I'll return the favor. I read the bandit was a cousin of yours." Quinton drilled the man.

"And you reckon that makes me privy to some sort of knowledge as to the whereabouts of the jewels — or possibly even a conspirator?"

Quinton noticed a curious aspect to Wentworth's speech. While the man seemed to speak with an almost cultured accent, the western style of speech crept into his voice every so often. The lawyer, in step with his office furnishings, was putting on a front. In itself, that probably meant damn little, but combined with other facts maybe . . .

Quinton shrugged. "Let's just start by

saying there might have been something your cousin let slip that would aid me in my quest."

Wentworth puffed out a smoke ring and leaned back in his chair. "Your words are transparent, Mr Hilcrest, but a nice try at any rate. I'll tell you what I told everybody in this town when I arrived. They pegged me as guilty without the benefit of knowing me as well." He cast Quinton a glare. "I had planned on coming here at the behest of the bandit's kin. They suspected he might have fallen in with a bad element and I was to try and set him on the straight and narrow, so to speak. By the time I made the arrangements, it was too late. He had been hanged for his part in the Black Hood crimes."

"So why come here, then, to a town you must have known would link you to the culprit?"

"The way you have linked me?"

The man was trying to intimidate him; he knew that and to an extent it was working. Wentworth had a way about him, one that would buffalo anyone not ready to deal with it.

"Let's call a spade a spade, Mr Wentworth. While I see the link as suspicious, I will give you a chance to explain yourself before rendering judgement."

"Well, now we have all our cards on the table, as they say. I'll tell you something, mister: I don't have to explain a damn thing to you or anyone, but the fact of the matter is I will. I came to this town to set the Wentworth reputation straight, to prove the name good in Hags Bend and undo any damage done by Calvin."

"Then what? I can't see much call for a man with your trade in Hags Bend."

"That's where you are wrong, Mr Hilcrest. Plenty of call. These folks always have some minor squabble and I proved right off to them they could depend on me to help them out."

"Offer them some free work to reel them in, then clean their pockets — that it, Mr Wentworth?"

Wentworth's face darkened a shade. "You have an annoying manner, Mr Hilcrest."

"I've been known to rub a few individuals the wrong way."

"I'm not surprised." A vaguely threatening note hung on the statement. "Well, Mr Hilcrest, you are right — to a point. I call it good sound business practice.

"I call it swindling."

Wentworth tensed, forcing himself to relax after a moment of silence. "I can tell you nothing about the missing jewels you probably don't already know." His tone turned abrupt.

Quinton caught the sudden finality in the man's words. He had pushed too hard. He stood, setting his derby atop his head.

"It's been a pleasure, Mr Wentworth. I'm sure we'll have the opportunity to talk again real soon."

"I feel sure of it." Wentworth's eyes bored into him.

"One last thing, Mr Wentworth. I have it from a reliable source that the deputy is a relative of yours."

"That's right, a nephew. Surely you're not implying a fine lawman such as — "

"Perish the thought." Quinton wondered if he had kept the lie out of his voice. "Just hear he takes up with some, how shall I phrase it, women of questionable reputation."

"My nephew's peccadilloes don't concern me, Mr Hilcrest. We all have our weaknesses, don't we?"

"Yes, we do." Quinton closed the door behind him.

He had learned one thing: Wentworth's presence in Hags Bend, in his mind, was questionable. He would not hand the lawyer the slack Molly had, not by any means. Wentworth was hiding something, Quinton felt sure, but what? And did that help him in his quest for the jewels? At this point he had further leads. Did Wentworth know anything about the jewels? That was far from being proved. The man impressed him as ruthless and overbearing and Quinton doubted he could make enough in lawyer's fees in this town to afford all the expensive furnishings in his office.

Quinton shoved the thoughts into the back of his mind, gathering up the reins and leading the bay along the street. Another point plagued him, something gnawing at the back of his thoughts since his ride to the cemetery, something he knew he had no business thinking.

Are you crazy?

He shook his head. He was. He had to be. Because instead of his task of finding the jewels, the most nagging thing on his mind was the lovely chestnut-haired woman he had met on the trail. Dash it all! He didn't even know her name! And he certainly didn't need the grief that went with courting! Hadn't he had enough of that with Dora? He would have thought so. But her face rose in his mind, smiling, lovely blue-green eyes glowing.

What had she said? Something about the town saying things about her? If that were true, Quinton knew who would know.

Maybe it was the detective's curiosity in him, or more likely it was plain knot-headedness, but he had to know more about her.

★ ★ ★

The Weeping Willow held only a few customers. The Durham haze had thinned, but the sour-whiskey smell was still strong. He paused inside the door, drawing a disparaging look from the two cowboys Deenie had sicced on him. He wondered why the sheriff had decided against keeping them locked up. Although both eyed him with thinly concealed fury, neither made a move to accost him as he approached the green-felt-covered table at which Chuck-a-luck sat. Deenie presented him with a snub and strode off; he felt just as glad for it.

"Find anything?" Chuck-a-luck looked up as Quinton pulled out a chair. The gambler clacked dice in his hand.

Quinton set the derby on the table and nodded. "Maybe. But I can't figure out what it means yet. Connections with no junction, that sort of thing."

"Told ya. No one'll ever find them jewels, son. Not you, not the next poor slob who comes in a lookin' and not the one after that. They's gone."

"Thanks for the vote of confidence."

"I'm a realist, son. When I gamble I damn well know how my luck's runnin'. I know when I'm gonna keep on losin'."

"Does it stop you from trying?" Quinton arched an eyebrow.

Chuck-a-luck crinkled his flat nose. "Awright, you got me there. But I get the feelin' you got it all staked on this last roll of the dice and if it comes up snake eyes . . ."

Quinton felt doubt gnaw at him again. Chuck-a-luck had hit it on the

119

mark and it made him uncomfortable, like knowing a dream was melting away.

"It'll work; I know it will." Quinton stated it with false confidence.

"For your sake, I hope so, son. I'd hate to see you end up buzzard bait. West ain't too forgivin' of tenderfeet who ain't got the sense to put their boots on when the trail gets rocky."

Quinton ignored the remark and glanced at the cowboys, who averted their gazes. "What are Deenie's admirers doing free? Thought the sheriff was going to let them cool off for the night."

Chuck-a-luck grunted, "Was. 'Cept he had to go to Casper Ridge on business. Deputy let 'em out."

"That surprises me." Quinton laid on the sarcasm. He went silent, running a finger over his upper lip, thoughts shifting from the two men to the woman on the trail. Good judgement almost got the better of him and he considered keeping quiet.

"What's on your mind, son?" Chuck-a-luck asked with a grin. "I can tell that look. Wouldn't be much of a gambler if I couldn't."

"Thought you lost a lot?"

"That's beside the point."

Quinton hesitated. "When I went to the cemetery earlier, well, there was a woman on the trail . . . "

"Oh-oh." Chuck-a-luck's lips twisted into a disapproving frown. He ran a hand through his bristly hair.

"I take it you know her?"

"You take it right. Stay away from her, son. Save yourself a bushel full of grief."

Too late for that, Quinton thought, but asked, "What do you mean?"

"You ain't gonna let me out of this, are you?"

"Not likely. It's the detective in me. Have to follow my instincts."

"Umm, more like what makes a losin' gambler keep playin' against the odds, I'm bettin'." Chuck-a-luck hesitated, leaning back in his chair. "Awright, but don't say I didn't warn yous. Her name's Turquoise and she's a galldamned witch! Least accordin' to this town."

Quinton savored the name in his mind. Turquoise. It fitted. Her lovely blue-green eyes . . . but what was the rest — "A witch? Balderdash! No such thing!"

"You listen to the talk goin' 'round Hags Bend and you might not be so sure."

"Talk is just that, talk. What makes her a witch?"

"Well, for one, she's always in that old cemetery, haunts it like a ghost, she does."

"So? I saw flowers on the boy's grave: maybe that's why she goes there. That doesn't make her a witch."

"Nope, it doesn't, but . . . "

"But what? You'll have to give me something more concrete than mere rumor."

"Well, she lives up there all alone in that little ol' cabin. Has since her folks passed on 'bout six years back. She makes these little dolls, devil dolls my gambling pardner, Freddy, calls 'em. Some kind of Indian things. Hear she puts spells on folks with 'em."

Quinton cast him a sceptical look. "Surely you don't believe that?"

"Don't know what I believe, but weird things happen to those who come in contact with her. Folks plain stay clear of her, now."

Quinton folded his arms. "What type of weird things?"

"Well, just that any man who gets near her finds his watch stopped, rumor has it." Chuck-a-luck eyed the gold chain dangling from Quinton's vest. "Checked lately?"

"Oh, come now. What rot!"

"Think so? Take a look at your piece and see. Bet it's stopped."

Quinton sighed and shook his head, tugging his watch from his pocket. His face pinched.

"What'd I tell ya? Bet that's about the time you saw her, too!"

It was and the hands had stopped. He tapped the face and they started moving again. After adjusting the hands to the proper time, he shoved it back in its pocket.

"That proves nothing! This old piece is always stopping on me. Haven't had the spare money for a new one."

"Maybe so, but I wonder. You'd just better take my advice and stay away from her. Witch or no, she's trouble. Any woman is!"

"That one point we can agree on, my friend."

"But it ain't gonna stop you, is it?"

Quinton grinned.

★ ★ ★

Bord and Ted watched the fancy-suited gent leave the barroom after talking to that no-good gambler, Chuck-a-luck. Bord's face twisted with hate. He gulped the whiskey in his glass and eyed his partner.

"I still say we should just bushwhack him and show 'im he can't get away with what he did."

Ted snorted. "An' have the sheriff throw us in the hoosegow for good? Where's your brains at, Bord?"

"You didn't look none too manly laid out 'crossed the floor, neither!"

Ted's face reddened. "Hell of a lot more than gettin' my britches hauled through a winder!"

"Awright, awright, we won't get nowhere fightin' with each other. I got me a notion."

"I'm afraid to ask . . . " Weariness hung in Ted's voice.

"You heard the way he was askin' about that woman up there in the woods?"

"The witch?"

"Witch, smitch! Bunch of local hogwash. Fact is, she's right fine lookin' and I been thinkin' about payin' her a visit myself for some time now. Maybe courtin' her."

Ted bellowed a laugh and slapped

the table. "You're loco! You know that? Plumb loco!"

Bord's face stained red. "Yeah? Well, you cain't see Deenie ain't never gonna give us the time of day, you stupid cowchip!"

Ted pushed out his chest. "Says you. I think she's got herself a hankerin' for me."

"Didn't look that way when she was steppin' on the back of your head!"

Ted clamped his mouth shut, hand going to the back of his head to massage the tender lump there. "You're a damn fool, Bord. You'll just get yourself cursed. You'll see. That woman's a devil woman!"

"Don't tell me you believe that bullspit? You jest wait. When I come back here with that pretty filly on my arm — "

"If you come back at all."

Bord hammered a fist on the table and shoved back his chair. He stalked from the barroom, leaving Ted shaking his head.

5

A WITCH! How ridiculous! It amazed Quinton that in this day and age, an age of the electric light and motor car, inoculation and phonographs, anyone could believe in such balderdash. Astonishing. Simply — well, he refused to believe it.

As Quinton guided his bay along the hard-packed trail, he blew a prolonged sigh. The talk didn't matter to him anyhow. He couldn't get the chestnut-haired young woman out of his mind and had spent half the night up thinking about her. Witch or no, he intended to visit her again. She had invited him back on the prerequisite that he hear the rumors, hadn't she?

Well, not exactly, but close enough for him.

You're a damn fool, that's what you are, Quinton Hilcrest!

He admitted he probably was. The last thing he needed was to be thinking about, let alone visiting, a woman when his life depended on finding the Black Hood jewels. Ludicrous, not to mention ill-timed and damned poor judgement.

At least some things hadn't changed in coming West. Once a fool . . .

Where had he gotten in his search for the jewels, anyway? Dead ends, vague links that dried up like the mist in the morning sun. He had virtually nothing to go on except a tale told in a less than reliable dime novel. Those jewels might just as well have been spirited away by squirrels, for all he knew. Squirrels liked shiny things, didn't they? The image brought a face to mind: Norvell Wentworth. All right, so he suspected the lawyer and his nephew deputy. So what? He couldn't back it up with proof. That left him checkmated in one respect, hopeful in another.

Black side: he couldn't prove

Wentworth or the deputy knew anything about the jewels. By the same token, the town couldn't prove the woman with the stunning blue-green eyes was a witch — white side. Though the two didn't relate, it left him an option to follow, if the wrong one.

He'd be disappointed again. That he might. Turquoise didn't strike him as the type who wanted or needed company, especially from the likes of a man who staked everything left to his name on a whim. He couldn't blame her, what with the story Chuck-a-luck had told him. She was an outcast, but perhaps that meant they had something in common.

You look for the strangest damn silver linings, Quinton, my man!

The bouncing of the horse brought him from his thoughts. The ride felt miles longer than it had the previous day and he was relieved when the tiny cabin came into view. He drew up and dismounted, tethering his bay to the hitch post. Smoke curled from the stove pipe and chimney; a woodsy scent, smoky-sweet, perfumed the air. Feeling his belly flutter, he drew a deep breath and went to the door, knocking. No answer. His hopes sank. She wasn't home. He had ridden up here for nothing and, dash it all, it was just a pipe dream, a whim.

Maybe she had gone to the cemetery. With smoke coming from the cabin she couldn't have wandered too far, could she?

A sound caught his attention and his hopes brightened. Splashing noises, coming from the back. He stepped off the porch, removing his derby and walking around the cabin. The ground, clustered with trees aflame with fall color, sloped towards the stream. It presented a serene setting and he could see why a woman such as Turquoise would prefer it, outcast or no. Turquoise. The name rolled off his mind and on to his tongue and he whispered it. A beautiful name.

"Oh my God!" he blurted before

he could stop himself, jerking to a halt as he came around a stand of trees. He spotted her stepping out of the stream; the sight froze him to the spot. He realized he was staring, mouth hanging open like the door to a coal stove. She was utterly beautiful, more beautiful than anything he could have ever imagined.

"Well, are you gonna stand there gawkin' or hand a lady her clothes?" She cocked an eyebrow and nudged her head to her clothes, which draped over a tree branch.

His mouth made fish movements. "Ah, ah, ah, you're ah, nah-nah-nah — "

"Naked," she finished. "Generally am when I take a bath. Fact, I was even born that way — wait, don't tell me, you came out fully clothed. Musta been right rough on your mama!"

His mind went blank. Weakness shivered through his legs and he knew if he didn't move within the next few seconds he might pass clean out and that would make quite an impression, indeed. With shaky hands he grabbed her clothes and handed them to her as if he were handing a bear its dinner.

"Well, you could at least turn around!" She held her clothes across her body and he stuttered something, God knew what, and turned, almost losing his balance and falling on his face in the process. He heard her chuckle and his face flushed.

A moment later she stepped past him and walked towards the house, stopping to look back when he didn't move.

"Well, now that we know each other up close and personal you might as well come in and have a cup of tea."

"Yes, yes, ma'am . . . " He trailed after her, managing to stumble over every rock and bulging tree root.

The cabin interior, warmed by a low fire, was cozy. Handmade blankets and crafts adorned the small room that served as parlor, kitchen and bedroom. On a bench by the south window rested a number of odd dolls, some half-completed. Indian work from the look of it, all exquisitely detailed.

"Those the devil dolls I heard about?" he asked, forgetting his tact at the door. He was still flustered and thinking about something before it tumbled out of his mouth was likely out of the question.

She turned, holding a copper teapot, and walked to the fireplace, setting it on a rack. A slight smile flittered across her lips.

"You're a brave man, Mr — "

"Hilcrest. Call me Quinton."

"Mr Hilcrest." A sarcastic gleam sparked in her eye. "You've heard the talk and yet you still dared to come here."

"Never been much for rumors, ma'am. Guess it goes with the job. Always check the facts before drawing conclusions."

"And what job is that, Mr Hilcrest? Staring at naked ladies fresh from their baths?" She grinned and went to the bench cluttered with dolls.

Heat flooded his face. "Sorry, I didn't realize . . . "

"I imagine."

She picked up a doll and ran her slim fingers over the hair, smoothing it, then setting the doll back on the bench. "Blackfeet, Crow, Cheyenne, Teton Sioux, each true to the tribe. I make them for a supplier back East. He sends a man to collect the newest batch every month or so. Sells them in fine shops. Guess they don't mind witches so much in New York." She eyed him mischievously and he got the impression she used a sense of humor to cover the fact that the talk bothered her. He made a note to watch his mouth in the future.

The teapot shrieked and she went to it. Pouring them each a cup, she handed him one and gestured to the sofa. He sat while she lowered herself into a chair.

"There's more talk, you know." She took a sip of tea.

"Tell you the truth, I don't pay much attention to that sort of thing."

"You don't now, but after you're here for a while it'll start to eat at you the way it did the rest of the townsfolk."

"Suppose you tell me first." He sipped his tea, noting a flowery bitterness and fragrance to it.

She smiled. "Don't worry, it's not poisoned. It's jasmine. The doll buyer brings it for me from a place called Chinatown. It's my favorite."

"Never thought for a minute — "

"Doesn't matter, Mr Hilcrest." Her gaze flicked to the chain dangling from his watch pocket. "Keeping good time, is it?" A wry expression turned her lips.

He felt a twinge of unease. "Never has. Stops all the time, if that's what you're asking."

"You sure I didn't curse it, Mr Hilcrest? I've been known to stop 'em dead."

He forced a smile but wasn't quite

sure how to take her. She was teasing him, testing him for some clue as to his personality as a whole. He guessed this was one woman with whom bluntness, or more accurately, honesty, would be appreciated.

"True that when I reached town after seeing you yesterday I found it stopped, but I've been tapping it for years because it stops working all the time. I no more believe you stopped its movement than I believe I won't find what I came to Hags Bend to find."

"Let me guess, the Black Hood jewels."

He blinked. "How'd you know?"

"I'm a witch, remember?" She laughed and there was more ease in the expression this time. "Not a long stretch, Mr Hilcrest. Whenever a stranger comes to town, chances are he's lookin' for the jewels. If I were a witch, I reckon I'da found them myself by now and left this . . . *place*, gone to New York or San Francisco, anywhere but here."

"I take it you have little love for this town?"

"Not since . . . " Her eyes grew distant, came back. "Well, not for a while, now."

He saw the sorrow sweep across her manner, stronger this time. Her gaze went to a tintype sitting atop the table next to her chair; it showed a boy of about ten or eleven.

"The cemetery . . . ?" Quinton's voice came low. He saw tears gather in her eyes and she set her cup on the table and lifted the tintype.

"My brother." Her voice held a tremble, a sadness that reached out and embedded his heart. He had the sudden urge to hold her, comfort her. "My parents died about six years ago. I was going to raise him, did for about a year. He . . . caught pneumonia . . . died . . . I miss him." She replaced the tintype, hands quivering.

"I noticed the flowers on the grave." His own voice fluttered. "I'm sorry."

"I go there every day, put new ones

down. Not to mention dig up bodies, as the town so kindly puts it."

"Doesn't matter what they say, ma'am. Take it from someone who's had a few rumors spread about himself." Bitterness laced his tone as he recalled the period following his discovery of Dora with another man, the things she had said and the people who believed her because she was a fine blue-blooded woman and him — a what? A nobody.

"Do you?" He couldn't tell whether it was a question or a challenge.

"Yes, I do. I was engaged to a woman, Dora, was her name. I found out . . . found out she had been taking up with another man, someone of higher stature than myself. I discovered later she was using me to make someone else jealous. She never really loved me and I suppose I should have seen it coming. What would a blue-blooded woman like that want with a man of low means such as myself?"

"We can't all be witches, Mr Hilcrest." The attempt at humor was genuine and warm. He felt himself relax.

Finishing his tea, he stood. "I should be going." She followed him to the door.

"Why did you come here, Mr Hilcrest? You don't strike me as the type to come merely to check out the local carnival attraction."

He met her gaze, almost losing himself in those stunning blue-green orbs. A glow started inside, spreading like wildfire.

"I came because . . . " He paused, lost for words. "I am not sure . . . right now, I'm not sure about a number of things." He stepped out, going to his horse.

"You could always come back sometime," he heard her say behind him as he mounted and reined around.

"I'd like that. I really would."

★ ★ ★

A mood wandered over Quinton that he couldn't place at first. It was unfamiliar, deeper than anything he had experienced with Dora. The glow inside blazed like the sun. All he could see in his mind was her face, her smile, and her sorrow. Turquoise had unnerved him, somewhat the way Dora had upon first courting, yet different. Turquoise had an honesty about her, a compassion that shone through the stone-wall exterior she kept up. But he had caught glimpses of her true emotions. She was used to being hurt; he could tell that. He was used to it as well and the fact cemented a bond between them that went even deeper than that. The swelling feelings made him question his true motivations and desires in life. He wondered what it would be like to marry a woman like that, cast away his silly notions of treasure and golden fleeces. Live a life where each day promised hard work and struggle, yet a certain comfort, a solidness, a reality never known to those who spent too much time dreaming.

He blew a prolonged sigh and swallowed at the emotion lodged in his throat. At the moment, the thought of hidden jewels and literary windmills seemed far away.

You are a fool, Quinton Hilcrest.

Maybe he was, but by damn if he could stop himself from plunging headlong into a raging river of possible heartache and disappointment.

At least he had that consistent factor in his life.

★ ★ ★

Turquoise hesitated at the iron gate leading to the cemetery. She clutched a bundle of fresh flowers and one of the little Indian dolls she made. A warrior. Tommy would like that.

With a deep breath she went in, leaves crackling beneath her bare feet, their scent ripe in her nostrils. It was still difficult to come here, even after all this time. The season made it worse. She despised this time of year. It reminded her of death, dying. Leaves leeched brown, decaying after blazing briefly with color, like the embers of a fire flickering out. Death and dying. Summer winds forced away by fall bluster, morning dew gone to hoar frost. The brilliant hazy sun sinking lower, becoming glaring and hard. Death and dying. Sickness and lost hope.

Emotion choked her throat and a sob escaped her lips. Tommy had died in the fall. Irrationally she blamed the season for it. It coddled bad memories and melancholy and she was damn tired of it.

Would she ever get over his death? Would she ever stop missing him? Would the time come when she wouldn't see his laughing face and smiling eyes and her heart would feel uplifted with the happiness her life had once held? She doubted it, at least now, even after the time that had passed. Some pain pierced too deep, pricked your soul, festered. On days like these she wished she was the witch the town made her out to be. Then she could bring him back, hold him again, take care of him.

Reaching his grave, she knelt and removed the dying flowers of the previous day, setting them aside and placing the fresh ones in front of the stone. She laid the doll atop the flowers. A tear whispered down her cheek.

"I miss you, Tommy." The words seemed lost in the breeze. She reached out and touched the carved letters of his name on the thin stone. The way she had a hundred times before. A day didn't pass she missed coming to his grave, telling him about her day, telling him she still loved him and thought about him, brought him the flowers. Maybe that meant she was dead as well, or at least empty, but she couldn't stop herself.

You have to let go, others had told her. Go on with your life. But how could she? Without him? What was there for her now? She supported herself making the dolls, her devil dolls, she thought with bitterness. She had nothing else in her life.

Or did she?

"I met someone today, Tommy." Another tear trickled over her cheek. "He's different, somehow. I think he's afraid of me, but not in the way the others in town are. I think he understands."

Quinton Hilcrest's face rose in her mind and she almost smiled. He was different. Handsome in a genteel way, not the rough-and-ready style of these western men. She reckoned he took baths regularly and not for a minute did he look at home on a horse. He appeared honest, to the point of being blunt perhaps, but that could be tempered and she much preferred it to the whispered accusations and disparaging looks of the men in Hags Bend. She could grow to love a man like that if she gave herself the chance, let herself live . . . she found herself

144

looking forward to the time he visited again.

If he visited again.

Would the rumors, the talk, wear on him, as it had the rest? she wondered. At first thought she was tempted to doubt it, but on second, why should she? Talk like that had a way of infecting folks. She found herself wishing he was different, stronger. He appeared to have the glint of a dreamer in his eyes. She remembered a time long ago when she could dream. Now —

A crackle of leaves snapped her reverie. She spun, straightening. A man stood behind her, a large man with a cruel face and a dagger of intent in his eyes that spoke of too much whiskey and too few scruples.

"Who are you?" she demanded, striving to keep her voice steady and hide the surprise and vague fear. "Why were you sneakin' up behind me?"

The big man grinned. "I knowed you come here ever'day, ma'am. Thought I'd come on up and pay my respects.

145

Name's Bord. I'm from town."

"If you're from town the last thing you'd be payin' is respects." Her tone sharpened. The man was up to something, but what? The visiting time, the same every day, was common knowledge. The town usually stayed clear of the cemetery during that time.

"I came to court you, ma'am."

She almost laughed, but something in his tone told her courting wasn't what he had in mind and taking no for an answer would not be likely. The notion chilled her, but she dared not let the fear show.

"I'm not interested in being courted, mister, so please step aside and let me pass!" She took a step to go around him but his hand shot up, clutching her arm, fingers gouging painfully.

"Cain't rightly do that, ma'am."

She stifled a bleat and her mind raced, looking for a way out of the situation. No one would come to her rescue, that was sure.

"Aren't you afraid I'll curse you?"

146

she said in desperation, hoping to use the town's fears against him.

He bellowed a laugh and the stench of sour whiskey slapped her face. "Hell, I ain't about to swaller that hogwash! Fact is, I've had my eye on you for some time now. I think we should spend some time gettin' acquainted — *ow*!"

She stamped a heel into his instep, satisfied by the sound of a brittle crack. The man released her arm and she followed the stamp with a slap across the face. She ran, not giving him time to recover and return the favor.

"Don't you worry, missy!" He yelled behind her. "I'll be payin' you another visit! Right soon, you hear?"

She didn't look back. She ran until she reached the cabin and bolted the door. Heart pounding, she reached beneath the bed and located her old shot-gun. Loading it, she gripped the stock with white hands. If he came back after her he'd be right sorry and leaking in his vitals.

* * *

In the cemetery, Bord touched his stinging cheek and groaned at the sharp stab of pain in his foot. Damn that sonofabitch witch! He would pay her another visit and show her a thing or two about proper manners when a man came a'courtin'! By damn he would. She had another thing comin' if she thought she could treat him that way and get away with it!

Bord stared in the direction she had taken, debating whether to go after her now or wait until she came back to the cemetery tomorrow. Maybe she had a weapon in the cabin. At the cemetery she'd be out in the open, easy prey. Besides, his foot hurt like hell and it'd be a damn long walk back to town on it. Better to wait.

Bord began walking with a limp, leaves crackling beneath his feet. Halfway through the cemetery, near the huge marble statue of an angel, he drew up. A noise had risen above the eggshell

148

crackle of brittle leaves, a grating —

The base of the statue opened!

He gawked as he saw the dark maw leading down into the ground, heard footfalls on stone echoing from the interior. A man appeared, features shadowed.

"You!" Bord said, mouth gaping. "What the hell are you doing in — "

Bord's mouth clamped shut as a blast sounded. He stared down at the crimson rose blossoming on his chest. Blood streamed between clutching fingers. Then blackness crushed him like a boulder.

6

"I HAD to kill him!" Deputy Jenson spread his hands, as he turned from the window to face Norvell Wentworth. Wentworth targeted him with a condescending expression and a spark of anger in his eyes.

"You took a fool chance! What if there had been somebody else around?"

"There wasn't."

"There damn well could have been! For cryin' out loud that girl goes up to the cemetery every day!"

Look, Bord gave me no choice. He saw me comin' outa the place. What was I s'posed to do, ask him politely to keep it to himself? No one else has a clue where them jewels and hidden money is and I'd as soon keep it that way."

Norvell Wentworth sighed and ran a hand over his jaw. "I reckon you're right, but you'd better be sure no one can tie us to it — especially the sheriff or that new guy, Hilcrest. He came here askin' after the jewels. I get the feeling he didn't believe a single word I said. What's more, I think he suspects you. You shouldn't have even come here in broad daylight."

Jenson grinned. "What? A deputy has no reason to visit the town's only lawyer? Don't worry, I made sure no one could tie us to it. That witch left one of her little devil dolls on the boy's grave, so I stuck it to Bord's body when I strung him up."

"What about the bullet hole in his chest?" Wentworth cocked an eyebrow.

"Worse comes to worse I'll sneak up and plant one of the guns at her place, somewhere obvious but not so obvious. I used one of the Black Hood guns. Was gonna pawn it, but now . . . "

Wentworth grumbled. "I still don't like it. We'll have to fence the jewels at a faster pace. I'll see if my man can handle more."

"Them jewels are kinda obvious. If too many crop up at once . . . "

Wentworth nodded. "I realize that, but I see little choice. We're bound to be seen sooner or later. That girl goes there every day and Hilcrest . . . "

"What about them?" Deputy Jenson's face darkened, viciousness gleaming in his eyes. "I could kill her just as easy. Then we wouldn't have to worry."

"No. Till now there's been no killin' and I don't aim to have a bunch of unexplained bodies lyin' around. That'll raise questions and I don't like questions. The town ain't likely to listen to her, even if she was to come in with some story about the statue. They think she's a witch. You said you pinned a doll to Bord's body, let's just see where that takes it. The town might get stirred up enough at that to save us the problem of dealing with her."

"And Hilcrest?"

"Mr Hilcrest is an entirely different matter. I know little about his methods, but he's got an eye for people. If he starts digging around it could mean trouble."

"Kill him?" Jenson looked eager.

"No, not yet. It'll look mighty suspicious if he turns up dead right after Bord. We don't need Presby snooping around either. Scare him for now."

"How?"

Wentworth shot him a bitter stare. "That's your expertise. Find a way and make sure no one sees you do it."

The door burst open and both men cranked their heads. Deenie stepped in, shutting it behind her.

"Oh, great!" Wentworth seemed to deflate. "Why don't we just put out a sign saying 'Jewel thieves, enquire here'?"

Deenie giggled and went to the deputy, sliding a hand over his cheek. "Don't you worry, now honeybun," she said to Jenson. "Too early for anyone to see me and if they did, what the hell? I get around . . ."

"So I've heard," Wentworth said sarcastically. He eyed Jenson. "What about the sheriff? He'll be gettin' on you if he sees you hanging with, with . . . *that*." He nodded at Deenie.

"Well!" Deenie turned up her nose. "Some folks just don't know respectable when they see it!"

Deputy Jenson chuckled. "Don't worry, he got a tip about the body hanging from a maple a mile or so from the cemetery. He's out there right now checkin' it out. Imagine it'll keep him busy a spell."

Wentworth looked back to the girl. "What the hell do you want?"

A smile oiled her lips. "Just protectin' my investment, sugar. Saw my beau here come by and reckoned I should be in on it."

"We're partners, you know," said Jenson. "Wouldn't do you no good to forget that." The threat in his voice was blatant.

Wentworth frowned. "You just remember who told you about the jewels in the first place. If it weren't for my inside information on the Black Hoods you never would have known where to find the jewels."

"Your cousin neglected to tell you where they were hidden, if I recollect right. I found 'em!"

"Based on my work. If Hilcrest makes the same connection we'll go down together."

"He won't. He don't look like so much to me. After I finish puttin' a scare into him he'll high-tail it back East so fast his britches will smoke!"

"Don't underestimate him, honey-bun." Deenie looked serious. "He looks like a drink of water but I saw him take out Bord and his buddy with his fancy fightin'. He's trouble. Heard he's got some soft spot for that witch, too."

"Oh wonderful, just wonderful!" Wentworth shook his head. "This is getting worse by the minute."

"You worry too much, Norvell," said Deputy Jenson.

"Somebody has to."

Deputy Jenson laughed, moving to the door. "You leave that witch and Hilcrest to me. I'll see to it they don't get any closer than they are — or face the consequences."

★ ★ ★

Quinton stepped from the hotel, filling his lungs with moist warm air. Rain had soaked the ground during the night; sunlight sparkled from puddles and glinted from bloated water troughs. A ghost mist haunted the ground in places and everything carried a clean earthy scent. Far different from what he was used to in the East, where rain snaked in rivulets across the cobblestones, amplifying the harsh sounds of early morning bustle: clacking hansoms and hammering hooves, the tap-tap of bootheels. Here it left a serenity, an aura of newness and promise. Of course, it might well have been chilly and damp and Quinton would have cared little at this point. His mind was too full of Turquoise and his swelling ardor.

He had lain awake a good portion of the night thinking about his visit to her cabin and when he had slept she had filled his dreams. He recognized the feeling, that headlong plunge down an emotional grain-shoot, but hadn't the good sense to stop it. The only thing on his mind was seeing her again.

You should be thinking about hidden jewels and what'll happen if you don't find them.

The thought intruded on his mood and he frowned. He needed to push on with his goal. What interest would Turquoise have in a man like him if he didn't come through on at least one dream in his life? Something told him it wouldn't matter to her, that she was as far-removed from Dora as a woman could be, but it didn't quell the little voice of doubt inside telling him he was setting himself up for another disappointment, perhaps two at once.

A shout shattered his reverie. He

157

looked in the direction of the saloon, seeing Chuck-a-luck ambling towards him.

"Top of the morning to you, Chuck-a-luck!" Quinton tipped his derby.

Chuck-a-luck halted, cocking an eyebrow. "You're in a mighty fine frame of mind for someone gamblin' his life on a dime-novel story."

"Ah, but when everything's right with the world even the petty annoyances don't matter."

Chuck-a-luck spat a disgusted sound. "God-almighty, you're stuck on her!"

Quinton beamed, aware that the expression looked ludicrous but unable to control himself.

Chuck-a-luck sighed. "Never mind, I got my answer. You best be keepin' an eye open, son. That gal's trouble. Especially after what I just heard."

The smirk plunged from Quinton's face. "What happened?"

He saw from the serious cast of Chuck-a-luck's face it wasn't good.

"Just that Bord was found murdered

158

'bout a mile from the cemetery, not too far from that gal's cabin, in fact."

"So? He didn't strike me as the sort to make any friends. I imagine more than one man had it in for the chap."

"Or woman . . . they found him hangin' from a tree. Big hole in the middle of his chest, too and one of her devil dolls stuck in his belt."

Quinton felt dread sink in his belly. On the face of it, it was circumstantial; it meant nothing, but in a town like Hags Bend, well, he had heard of lynchings done on far less evidence than that.

"I have to go to her," Quinton said. "She might need a detective's help."

"Son, I'd head the exact opposite direction if'n I was you. You'll just bring a heap of trouble on yourself."

Quinton's brow furrowed. "It's the last hand in a poker game and you get a hand that's borderline. You've been losing all night and you could fold but the other guy looks to be bluffing. Do you play your hand?"

Chuck-a-luck sighed. "I play, but I know better."

"So do I."

Quinton went to the livery stable and secured his horse. As he led him out into the street, he noticed a wagon rumbling in from the trail. Passing it, he spotted a blanket-covered form bouncing about in the back. Bord? It had to be. A stab of dread skewered him. What if the rumors were true? What if she . . . ?

Don't be ridiculous! he scolded himself. He knew better than to let idle gossip mar his judgement. Yesterday he had judged Turquoise to be a caring, loving, beautiful woman. He'd stick with that.

He stepped into the saddle, groaning as his backside bitched from the previous day's riding. Gigging the bay into a canter, he headed down the trail.

Deeper ruts grooved the trail today, tracks gouged by wagon wheels, puddles making the earth spongy in places. He should have taken it more cautiously, given his inexperience in riding, but his thoughts were focused on Turquoise and the trouble she might be in.

The cabin came into view and he breathed a sign of relief. The sigh became a gasp.

The thunder of a gun blast jolted him. He tightened his hold on the reins, hands bleaching. Something shrieked past his ear and with a sudden plunging sensation in his being he realized it was a bullet.

At the moment that seemed the least of his problems.

With the blast the horse jerked to an abrupt stop and reared. Its hooves beat the air as it neighed in fright. The saddle and his rear suddenly parted company.

He got the momentary sensation he was somehow flying — until the ground rushed up to remind him people didn't fly and he was no exception.

He slammed into a puddle face-first

with a bone jarring jolt and a splash. Muddy water filled his mouth, clogged his nose and soaked his clothes.

The bay bounded off towards the cemetery.

As soon as the drumming in his ears subsided, Quinton took a moment to take stock of his person and make sure no bones had been broken. None were, though he knew once the shock wore off he'd be sore in more places than he could count.

"If you're gonna come callin' on a lady, Mr Hilcrest, least you could do is do it on your feet . . . "

A voice penetrated the buzzing of his head and he lifted his gaze to look up at the woman standing over him.

He grunted something and spat mud. She shook her head and chuckled, then bent to help him up. "Reckon you ain't had much experience on a horse," she said, leading him towards the cabin.

His legs wanted to go in different directions at first, but steadied as he walked. For the moment he kept the gunshot to himself, eyeing the sides of the trail suspiciously.

She guided him to the stream. "Wait here," she said, hurrying back to the cabin and returning a few moments later with a bundle of pink cloth.

"Take off your clothes, Mr Hilcrest," she said, eyeing the stream.

"What?" he stammered, face turning red.

"They're full of mud. I can't very well wash them with you still wearing them, can I? 'Sides, we'll be even then." She smirked. "Here, you can put this on. Sorry, it's the only thing I had." She unraveled a pink bathrobe.

"You've got to be kidding?" he said meekly.

She shook her head, grin widening.

★ ★ ★

"I feel stupid as all get-out in this!" grumbled Quinton, sitting by the fire in the pink bathrobe.

She laughed, draping his wet clothes

163

over a rack near the fire. She had scrubbed them with hard soap in the stream and even darned a small hole he'd opened in the knee. After, she'd fixed him a cup of tea. While he felt embarrassed he also felt something else; a closeness to her that was entirely too comfortable.

"Someone took a shot at me," he said bluntly, as she lowered herself on to the sofa. "That's why I was thrown."

Shock crossed her face. "Are you — ?"

"I'm fine. Just fell on my pride." He tried to grin and the worry on her face eased. "I think somebody just wanted to scare me or I'd be dead."

"Why should anyone want to do that?"

He shrugged. "Maybe I ruffled someone's feathers. I've managed to irritate a few people since I arrived in Hags Bend. Take your pick; the deputy, Bord and Ted, from the saloon, Deenie, or Norvell Wentworth."

"Is that reason enough to shoot at you?"

"Maybe I stumbled on a link to the jewels and maybe whoever it is came down with a case of the worries." The idea made sense to him. He had stepped on a toe and someone had yelped. But who?

"If someone was warning you, Mr Hilcrest . . . " — she stood, walking to the window and peering out. Her voice lowered — "maybe you should leave before something worse happens. Their aim might improve next time."

"Do you want me to leave?"

She didn't answer, merely kept her gaze focussed on some distant spot.

"I came here for a reason; I intend to finish what I started." He said it with more confidence than he felt. Back East he had never once been shot at, though God knew every other manner of bad luck had befallen him. The breath of danger on his neck made him uneasy yet excited at the same time.

"Is it worth it?" Turquoise turned from the window, blue-green eyes intense. "Is the recovery of those jewels worth losing your life over?" The intensity of her eyes melted to pain and he saw a grim reflection of loss and death. "I've staked everything I own on this trip, Turquoise, though it doesn't seem to matter as much to me as it once did. I have another reason for sticking around."

A smile filtered on to her lips. He pretended to sip his tea, feeling his face heat.

She remained silent and Quinton's expression turned serious as Chuck-a-luck's news invaded his mood. There was still the matter of a dead man, wasn't there? He drew a breath and caught her gaze.

"I need to ask you something, Turquoise. I'm not quite sure how."

"You strike me as an honest gent, Mr Hilcrest. Say it straight out. That's the best way."

"OK . . . a man was found murdered

166

down the trail, not far from here from what I was told. Too close to the cabin the way the town sees it. Someone found him hanging from a tree with a hole in his chest and one of your dolls in his belt."

A gasp parted her lips. "Who?"

"Big guy, name of Bord from the saloon. Don't know what he was doing up here — "

"I know . . . " Her voice lowered. She came over and fell into the sofa. "Yesterday, he came to the cemetery while I was putting flowers on Tommy's grave. He made . . . advances. I slapped him and ran off."

"The doll?" He let his detective training take over. He needed to know everything.

"I made it for Tommy. I left it on the grave with the flowers. Bord must have picked it up."

"I guessed it was something like that." He hoped the relief didn't show in his voice. While he had not doubted her, hearing it from her lips made him feel better about the situation.

"Guessed. Or do you mean hoped?" She eyed him as if searching for any hint of a lie.

"I *knew* it. I'm not like the others in Hags Bend. I may be a lot of things, but I know people. I have to in my line of work and I know you haven't got it in you to kill anybody."

"Thank you, Mr Hilcrest . . . *Quinton*. I needed to hear it from you."

After a moment of silence, he asked; "Did you notice anything unusual while you were at the cemetery?"

"No, nothing." She hesitated and he sensed something else on her mind.

"You're leaving something out."

"It's probably nothing, just some- times . . . "

"Sometimes what?" He moved to the edge of the chair.

"Sometimes I get the feeling, nothing more than that, mind you, that someone's watching me while I'm there, someone I can't see."

"Ever see anyone?"

"No, never. But I've heard *sounds* a few times."

"What kind of sounds?"

"Grating sounds, like something heavy being moved. Footsteps on dry leaves. But when I turn around . . . there's nothing."

Quinton slid a finger across his upper lip. "The more I hear the more everything leads back to the cemetery."

"I saw the sheriff ride that way earlier. Now I know why."

As if in response, a knock hammered on the door and Turquoise started. They glanced at each other, then the door.

"Had a feeling he'd get around to you sooner or later," Quinton said, frowning. "Guess it was sooner."

She stood and went to the door. Sheriff Presby, hat in hand, filled the doorway.

"Mornin', ma'am. Mind if I come in a moment? Got myself a few questions I need answered."

"Not at all, Sheriff." She stepped aside and motioned him in. As Presby stepped through the doorway, his gaze locked on Quinton, who looked anything but dignified sitting in a chair wearing a pink bathrobe.

"You manage to get around, Mr Hilcrest," Presby said with a frown. "I ain't even gonna ask 'bout your choice of attire . . . "

Quinton felt like sinking into the chair, but forced a bravado. "Someone took a shot at me on my way up here this morning. I was thrown from my horse into a puddle. My clothes are drying."

The sheriff nodded and Quinton couldn't tell whether he believed the story.

"Lots of shooting goin' on in these parts, seems like. Fact, ma'am," he turned to Turquoise, — "fella got himself shot up then hung a short piece from your place. Wouldn't know anything about that, would you?"

She shook her head, lips tight, hands

170

clenched till her knuckles bleached. "Mr Hilcrest just told me of it. That's the first I knew."

"How'd you come across that information?" Presby eyed Quinton.

"Chuck-a-luck told me. Like they say, news travels fast in Hags Bend. Guess it works two ways."

Presby nodded, but his thoughts seemed elsewhere. His gaze drifted to the doll table against the wall. He reached into a pocket and pulled out a doll, holding it up. "Ain't got the best eye for these things, ma'am, but strikes me this doll 'bout matches the ones on that bench." He nudged his head towards the bench.

"I made it for my brother." No hesitation impeded her voice and she straightened her carriage, chin coming forward. Good girl, Quinton thought, respect for her swelling. He admired her spunk. She wouldn't be pushed around by the lawman and that made her story all the more believable.

Presby pulled at an earlobe. "Found

it on the body. How you reckon it got there?"

"I have no idea. I left it on the grave."

"You know the dead man, fella by the name of Bord?"

"I'll tell you just what I told Quinton — Mr Hilcrest. He accosted me at the cemetery yesterday. I slapped him and ran off. He threatened to call again."

"That make you mad enough to kill him?" The question was meant to shake her composure, define whether she was telling the truth. She held her ground and Quinton smiled inwardly. "No, Sheriff, it didn't. But if he had come back I might have had to."

"You own a .45? Maybe a Colt?"

She shook her head. "I have a shotgun left me by my parents. That's all."

"Oh, come on, Sheriff!" Quinton stood and came towards them. "How could she possibly have shot him, then lifted him on to a horse, put a noose around his neck and then planted one of her own dolls on the body to point the way back here? That makes no sense! Even you can see that!"

The sheriff eyed him with a trace of venom. "If you weren't wearing a pink robe I'd consider busting you in the chops for that, Hilcrest. We might not have your fancy eastern detective ways in Hags Bend but I know my job. If I didn't figure right off there was somethin' damn suspicious 'bout it I would have been here soon as I cut the body down and escorted the lady to a nice clean cell. As it is, I got my doubts and I think I smell something rotten in the root cellar. But I'll do my job and ask my questions, whether you think they're sensible or not. You got any problem with that?"

"Ah, no, Sheriff. I'm sorry. I realize you have a job to do."

Presby set his anvil jaw. "I want to see you in my office later, that understood?" Quinton nodded. "By the way, there's a bay tied up at the cemetery. I assume it belongs to you."

The sheriff put on his hat and stepped to the door.

Looking back to Turquoise, he said, "I may need you to answer more questions, ma'am. Reckon that'll be all right with you?"

Turquoise nodded. "I didn't kill the man, Sheriff."

"Reckon I never said you did."

★ ★ ★

By the time Quinton's clothes had dried and he walked to the cemetery to retrieve his horse, the sun glared high in the sky and the ground had dried. Quinton rode back to town, mind tumbling with questions. The murder added a new and dangerous dimension to things, as did the attempt to scare him off. It meant his simple search for hidden treasure had turned into a live case. Forces were still at work, despite the demise of the Black Hoods. The bandits were dead and buried but someone, or ones, lurked behind the scenes. Another party searching for the jewels? Maybe. Or maybe they had already found them and didn't want the competition. That would explain the attempt to scare him off. But why kill Bord? Where did the ruffian fit in? Had he stumbled on to something? Turquoise said she had left him in the cemetery. All trails led there, but Quinton had thoroughly searched the bone orchard and come up empty. Still, there had to be something or Bord wouldn't be dead.

Another thought struck him: Turquoise went to the cemetery every day; that meant she was in danger — or had the problem been dealt with? Was someone worried she would discover something? Had that someone placed the doll on the corpse to implicate her, get her out of the picture? Whoever it was hadn't thought the thing through. No decent lawman would arrest Turquoise on that evidence. Too many intangibles existed. While the sheriff hadn't said it, Quinton could tell the lawman had thought of the possibility she had shot Bord after forcing him at gunpoint on to the horse. A shot would have sent the horse bolting and the noose tightening. The sheriff would save that point until other evidence showed up. For now, he'd leave her be.

Quinton drew up in front of the sheriff's office and stepped from the saddle. Tethering the bay, he went in, seeing Presby seated behind his desk and the deputy eyeing him from a chair.

"Afternoon, Sheriff." Quinton tipped his derby. "You wanted to see me?"

"Hilcrest." A disgusted note hung in the sheriff's tone. "You're like a can of bad beans, know that? Ever since you came into town I've had nothing but gas."

"I've been told I have that effect on some people."

"Don't surprise me, none."

Quinton went right to the point. "You didn't arrest her. Why?"

"Like I said, things about it don't

176

make sense and until they do I won't make a move on her. Reckon she's had enough grief from this town."

Quinton came closer to the desk. "She's no witch, Sheriff. She's kind and gentle and honest. Lots more than I can say for certain others in these parts." He shot a glance at the deputy.

The sheriff stared at him, cocking an eyebrow. "You're stuck on her, ain't ya?"

Quinton shrugged, non-committal.

Presby grinned. "Rumor has it she poisoned her brother, you know."

"Her brother died of pneumonia. Thought you didn't believe what the rest of these people do?"

"Don't, but that's the kind of talk you're gonna hear."

"I'm not concerned with it. I'm only concerned with her."

"Suit yourself." Presby ran a hand over his square jaw. "Took a look around on my way back to town. Found another set of tracks in the mud a ways down. Might belong to the fella you said shot at you."

"You believe me?"

"Till I know otherwise. Seems I ain't the only one who got a bad can of beans. Best watch yourself."

"I'll keep that in mind. That why you wanted me here, to warn me?"

"Basically. I'll admit you rub me the wrong way, but I ain't got a hankerin' to find you hangin' from a tree with a doll stuck in your belt. I'd as soon no one else was killed. One body's enough and I aim to find out who's responsible for it. I find myself a suspect I'm gonna take me a look at his horse. If it matches the prints I found along the trail, I say we got the man who shot at you and maybe murdered Bord."

"You checked my bay, I take it?"

"What kind of lawman would I be if I hadn't?"

★ ★ ★

Quinton left the office, a vague sensation washing over him of something off-kilter. He couldn't put his finger on it, but it bothered him. He felt sure the sheriff meant what he had said, that he would do his best to find the real killer, but . . .

It struck him; the deputy! This time Jenson had acted subdued, hadn't said a word, in fact. He looked — worried, vaguely; that was it. Was he the man who had taken a shot at him? Killed Bord? Quinton wasn't quite ready to go that far, but he had to be more careful. Whoever had shot at him would know he'd decided to ignore the warning and stay in town. Next time the bullet might come a whole lot closer.

At the moment, that didn't worry him as much as the possibility of danger to Turquoise. The same culprit would learn the sheriff hadn't arrested her. If she posed a danger to him . . .

For now Quinton felt moderately safe in thinking whoever set her up was trying to kill two birds with one body. If she was in immediate danger they would have killed her the way they did Bord. That they had bothered to set her up showed her to be more of an annoyance, a possible threat. He suspected it had something to do with her presence in the cemetery every day.

It left him without a lead, merely a bunch of suspicions and dangling threads. Sooner or later he was going to have to pull on those threads and see what unraveled.

7

"**I**'M getting close to something — someone took a shot at me today!" Quinton arched an eyebrow and cast Chuck-a-luck a confident look. He tossed his derby on the green-felted table and sat.

Few customers patronized the Weeping Willow. Quinton saw no sign of Bord's partner, Ted, or Deenie.

"You're close to gettin' your damn fool head blowed clean off!" The man's perpetually crooked expression became more twisted. He clacked a pair of dice in his hand.

"This was just a warning. If they had wanted me dead, I would be. I made an easy target and I wasn't expecting trouble."

"Just the same, it might be a good idea to take the warning and skedaddle 'fore you're cold as a wagon tire. I got a bad feelin' 'bout this, son, just like the ones I get right before I lose a whole pot after a winnin' streak — and before you go pointin' it out, yes, I still play it anyhows, but this ain't the same thing. I just lose eatin' for a week; you could lose your life. Hell, you ain't even carryin' a piece. That's unheard of in these parts!"

An indignant look crossed Quinton's face. "Not so, my good man. I am not totally unschooled in the ways of the West."

"Yeah? I don't see no gunbelt beneath that fancy suit, which I might add is lookin' a bit long in the tooth."

Quinton shot a look around the room, making sure they weren't being watched. He probed in a suitcoat pocket and brought out a derringer, holding it flat in his palm.

Chuck-a-luck guffawed and Quinton's face reddened. "Hell, son, that's a damn lady's gun! Lucky if you'd hit anything with that more than ten feet away. What's it got, two shots? You'd be dead an' buried 'fore you got the chance to use it!"

Quinton's lips tightened and irritation pricked him. He'd always considered the need for a gun minimal in his cases back East. The derringer was tiny and didn't show and he preferred that. He'd never had to use it and until now had seen no reason to opt for anything larger. But, thinking it over, he saw Chuck-a-luck's point. Things played by different rules out West, wild and unpredictable. The shot at him had proved that. At any moment, the unscrupulous forces at work in Hags Bend might decide he had become too much of a threat. What would happen if they, whoever they were, confronted him? Would he have to protect himself with more than kung fu? Would he get the opportunity to draw the peashooter, let alone use it? Doubt suddenly nagged him.

"OK," he said, spreading his hands. "I concede. Maybe I need something bigger."

183

"Glad to see you makin' some sense, son. This ain't the East. Things are different here. Death and justice can be swift. I'd hate to see you break an ankle 'fore you even got out the gate."

"I'll keep that in mind." Quinton paused, pocketing the derringer, then running a finger over his upper lip. "I think the same person wants Turquoise out of the way as well."

Chuck-a-luck gave a disgusted grunt. "I knew you'd get hung up on that gal!"

Quinton bristled. "So what if I am?"

"Look, I ain't sayin' the rumors about her are true, but fact is she's a loner, has been since her parents died, more so since her brother passed — some say she poisoned him, you know." Chuck-a-luck cocked an eyebrow.

"So I heard. He died of pneumonia."

"I know that, but the thing is the town don't see it that way. You take up with her and just as soon they'll be labeling you as the devil's own."

"What about you, Chuck-a-luck, you see it that way?" Quinton gave him a serious look and the gambler grinned.

"Hell, I always been one for a longshot and I reckon I'm too old to change now."

"Nice to know I can count on someone if I have to."

"Oh, you can count on me, but just recollect, I ain't got the longest winnin' streak you heard tell of. Fact, I lose more than I win, but I'm too bullheaded to stop myself!"

"Some people would say the same thing about me."

"So what's your next move, son? Where do you head from here?"

Quinton considered it before answering. What was his next move? He seemed checkmated. "Can't tell you for certain. I know what I suspect, but I can't prove any of it. Wentworth, the deputy, I think they're involved, though how I can't tell you, either. Do they know where the jewels are? Are they looking

185

for them same as I am? Will they kill me to stop me from finding them?"

"Sounds like you got lots more questions than you got answers. From a gamblin' standpoint that don't set the odds in your favor."

"No it does not. But it all seems to lead to one place: the cemetery. I think I'll have another looksee up there."

"That place's been gone over a hunnert times, but the sheriff, the deputy — "

"The deputy?" Quinton's brow crinkled.

"Yep, he spent quite a bit of time up there when he first got on the job. Said he thought he could find the jewels but never did."

"You sure of that?"

Chuck-a-luck shrugged. "Who can say? Ain't likely he'd make it public news if'n he did."

"You would have made a damn fine detective with an attitude like that, Chuck-a-luck."

"Couldn't do no worse at that than

I done at gamblin'!"

Quinton's face grew thoughtful. "Let's suppose for a moment the deputy did find the jewels. What would he do with them?"

"Give 'em back?" Sarcasm hung in Chuck-a-luck's voice.

"In a pig's eye! He'd get rid of them somehow, turn them into cash, probably over a long period of time so no one would become suspicious."

"Think that's what he done?"

Quinton shook his head. "I don't think he has the connections for that, nor the brains."

"You thinkin' . . . ?

Quinton nodded. "He got someone to do it for him, a partner perhaps."

"Wentworth?"

"Wentworth. Maybe he even knew where the jewels were all along."

Chuck-a-luck shook his head. "Can't see how. The bandits were both dead before Wentworth and the deputy moseyed into town."

Quinton agreed. "I read articles on

them. Said the sheriff killed one and hung the other. Still, seems if they hadn't found the jewels there'd be little reason to try to scare me off."

"'Less they was worried you might find them first."

Chuck-a-luck had a point, but Quinton's scent was tingling again. Perhaps it had been something in Wentworth's manner that labeled him as a man with more than a simple race to find a treasure on the line.

"What about the surviving bandit?" Quinton asked.

"What about him?"

"Sheriff said he hanged him, but the articles didn't give much about his background."

"Not much to tell. Was a local hardcase. Got in some minor scrapes with the law, but nothing major it seemed. Had himself a little place at the edge of town."

"Sheriff go over it? Find anything?"

"Nope, not a thing. Can of beans and some painted shells he got off

Molly, from what I heard. Not much else. Almost like he never really lived there. No personal belongin's, neither."

"Odd." A vague thought took shape in Quinton's mind. "Wonder if he could have been living mostly at the hideout."

"What hideout? No one ever found no place like that."

"Had to be one. Men don't just disappear into thin air and they certainly weren't ghosts. That means they needed a place to hide."

Chuck-a-luck ran a hand through his wire-brush hair. "Seems to me you find that, you find the jewels."

"My sentiments exactly. What about when the bandit was awaiting hanging, he say anything?"

Chuck-a-luck shrugged. "No idea. You might ask the sheriff or Molly; anyone knows, they would."

"I think I'll do just that."

"We got somethin' else to do first, son. It's time you got acquainted with the way of the West."

It took most of the money he had, but when Quinton and Chuck-a-luck left the gunshop he was a few ounces lighter in the wallet and a few pounds heavier at the hips. Chuck-a-luck had guided him in the purchase of a Colt Peacemaker .45, a huge gun, at least compared to the 'lady's gun' tucked in his pocket. Next, Chuck-a-luck dug up a spare gunbelt, which Quinton buckled around his waist. The gun felt as heavy as an anvil at his side and until he got used to the weight he walked decidedly sideways.

They went to a clearing at the edge of the woods at the edge of town, where Chuck-a-luck set up a line of bottles on a dilapidated fence rail. Brushing off his hands on his trousers, Chuck-a-luck ambled toward Quinton, eyeing him then the bottles. "Hit the blue one first, the yellow one second, the brown third."

"How many shots I get?" The

question drew a frown from Chuck-a-luck.

"You got a man in front of you aimin' a gun an' you got one shot; you'd best get it off first and true. Don't ask me no more stupid questions like that again!" He grinned crookedly and Quinton scrunched his face in disapproval.

Chuck-a-luck stepped back and Quinton squinted at the bottles fifty feet away. He spread his stance, aiming the Peacemaker. Nerves fluttered in his belly for some reason he couldn't pinpoint. He thumbed back the hammer.

The blast stunned his eardrums and the recoil kicked him backwards. He hit the ground on his rump. Hard. He looked up at the bottles, all still in line on the fence.

"You missed," said Chuck-a-luck, vague humor in his voice.

Quinton cast him a disparaging look. "Why didn't you tell me the damn thing would take my arm off?"

Chuck-a-luck's crooked grin widened.

"Some things are best learnt on their own. Now git up an' try again. This time I'll show you how to hold it."

It took his twenty shots to hit a bottle and by that time his arm felt numb, and his shoulder ached.

"There!" Quinton shouted, gesturing at the shattered bottle, proud despite the discomfort in his arm.

"Don't git too full of yourself, son. You got to hit each one on the first shot 'fore you can jump up and down."

"You're a breath of encouragement, Chuck-a-luck."

"Reckon I am, at that!"

★ ★ ★

The day had stretched into late afternoon by the time Quinton, Peacemaker at his hip, rode the trail towards the cemetery. He had reached a few conclusions. One, he needed a lot more practice before he acquired any skill with the Colt — if his arm didn't fall off first; two, before searching the cemetery again he needed to ask the sheriff or Molly about anything the robber might have let slip before getting his neck stretched, as the saying went in Hags Bend; three, he needed to keep his eyes open before he wound up with a third eye betwixt the two he already had — a lead eye; and last, he needed to see Turquoise again and tell her his feelings.

He'd given the last the most thought. The situation with the jewels had scared a sense of mortality into him. He could barely handle the 'iron' at his hip and ignoring the warning was an open invitation to getting killed.

The thought chilled him. He had to be ready for death. If he ran he would lose everything — the jewels, the reward and most importantly, Turquoise. If he stayed he chanced losing them in a more permanent settlement. It was a gamble and the odds for losing were . . .

Not encouraging.

That's when he had reached his

decision. If the worst happened he had to make sure Turquoise knew his feelings towards her. It was crazy, he knew, falling in love with a woman he had only met a few times. There was just something about her, something about him, and the two fitted together snug as a puzzle block. At least in his mind they did. Maybe her feeling would be, well, different . . . but after his experience with Dora he would lay his cards on the table. If his hopes were dashed it would be nothing new and he preferred it come at the beginning. Turquoise would be honest with him, he felt sure. If she felt the same way, he would gladly give up his quest for the jewels, grab a chance at a normal life. If not, well, finding the jewels was worth the risk, because he was back to square one with nothing but failure chasing him.

He wished the prospects appeared more cheerful than they did. The inevitability of events darkened his mood. He'd never been one to dwell on such possibilities, only on the dream. Now he was forced to face the reality at the end of the dream. For the first time in his life he was considering consequences. Maybe that was a good thing, but it tasted like medicine. It told him the only thing a windmill was good for was wind.

The cemetery came into view. Quinton had stopped first at the cabin, finding her not at home. He knew she could be at only one other place.

He drew up and stepped from the saddle, then tethered the bay.

Butterflies danced in his belly and his legs felt wobbly.

He spotted her kneeling before the grave of her brother. New flowers lay in front of the stone, the old ones placed on the side. She glanced up as leaves crackled beneath his feet. He saw tears trickling down her face and felt a sudden need to hold her, comfort her.

"I don't think I'll ever stop missing him, Quinton," she said, standing. "I thought it would get easier but it hasn't. I'd give anything to bring him back, trade places with him."

He swallowed, emotion clogging his throat. "I know you would but you can't. He wouldn't want you to. He'd want you to go on with your life, live it instead of dying inside."

"I can't forget him . . . he looked so, so fragile the day he . . . "

He stepped forward, taking her in his arms. It felt right, more right than any silver-coated dream ever had.

"You don't have to forget him, just live your life and keep his memory."

"It was so hard after he died. Every day seemed worthless. The sun still rose and set at night, but the time seemed . . . empty, lost somewhere till . . . "

"'Till what?" He drew back to look into her eyes. He saw the sadness there, the emptiness of a hundred days bleeding with pain and loss and hurt. It reached out, gripping him, flooding him with emotions he had never felt, even with Dora, especially with Dora. In that instant he realized he had never loved the eastern woman, only thought he had, searching for something that was only a dream the way everything else in his life was; a dream that dissolved when you tried to touch it. Until now.

" 'Till you came along," she said.

He kissed her full and she responded, her lips warm and beseeching. Both had been searching and both had found it with a kiss.

She pulled back suddenly, pushing him away and turning, a sob racking her body.

"What's wrong?" He took a step towards her. She turned to him, tears running down her face.

"I don't know if I can love you, Quinton. I don't know if I can love anyone any more. I think it all died with Tommy."

"It didn't die, Turquoise. You're just afraid to find out it didn't. You kept your love locked away so long it feels

197

like it isn't there. I know. I made myself believe I loved someone who didn't love me. I know now I was trying to hold on to something never there, because now I know what it truly is."

She turned away again, sobbing. "Please leave, Quinton. Please leave before I can't let you . . ."

"I want to stay with you."

"I need time . . ."

He felt his heart sink. "I think time's the one thing you've had too much of already." He started to walk away, halting and turning back to her. "I love you, Turquoise. If I haven't ever been sure of anything in my life I'm sure of that."

★ ★ ★

He was gone and like a fool she had let him walk away. She loved him; she was only fooling herself if he thought different. Love. It was foolish and impulsive and a feeling she had told

198

herself she would never have again. Love meant pain, losing. She had loved her parents and Tommy and she had lost them. If she let herself love Quinton . . . forces already conspired against him. Someone had taken a shot at him and next time . . .

If you love him, he'll die!

The thought was irrational but she couldn't stop it.

It's too late, you can't deny your feelings for him.

For the first time in years she wanted to let herself go, fill the emptiness that had swallowed her heart after Tommy died. Quinton offered her that chance and she sensed she offered it to him —

A footfall snapped her thoughts short. Leaves crackled as someone came towards her and for a moment she thought Quinton had returned. She turned, hopeful, the hope quickly dashed when she saw Hags Bend's deputy step around the base of a huge marble angel.

"What are you doing here?" she demanded, voice defensive. She felt embarrassed that he saw her crying, saw her vulnerable. It was a side she never showed anyone in town. She constantly fought to maintain a false front of toughness and devil-may-care where they were concerned.

"You ain't here at your regular time," the deputy said, a hint of anger in his tone.

"I had . . . company earlier!" She managed to put some sarcasm behind her voice.

"Sheriff should have arrested you, you know." The deputy took a step closer, a vicious glint sparking in his eyes. "You killed that fella, Bord. I know it. I'd have you hangin' from a cottonwood by now if it were up to me."

"Well, it's not up to you!" she snapped, feeling her strength rush back. "It's up to the sheriff and he's got a lot more sense. What are you doing here, anyway? I didn't hear you ride up."

"I . . . walked," he mumbled, a stumble in his voice. "Came up here to make sure nothin' was missed in that fella's murder."

"I don't believe you." She knew she should have kept that opinion to herself, but anger got the better of her.

"Don't rightly matter what you believe, missy. I aim to prove you killed that fella and when I do you'll look just as pretty hangin' from a rope. It's the least a witch like you deserves."

She didn't know what made her do it — the arrogance in his manner or her own annoyance at him witnessing her vulnerability — but she stepped forward and planted her bare heel in his kneecap. A crack sounded and he yelped, clutching his knee and blistering the air with words that shouldn't have been uttered in the presence of a lady. She ran off, leaving him cursing and yelling her name. By the time she reached her cabin, out of breath and exhausted, she found herself laughing for the first time in a long time.

8

"I'M tellin' you we have to do something about her!" Deputy Jenson shouted, leaning on Norvell Wentworth's desk with two fists. "She damn near broke my leg!"

"She see you come out of the place?" Wentworth's eyes narrowed. His face reddened.

"No, no, she didn't — but she coulda."

"That much you are right about, Jenson. She might well have seen you and that would have been too bad. We can't risk it any longer. We have to remove those jewels before she does."

"That's plain loco! Why not just give her the same treatment I gave Bord and be done with it?"

"You think that'd work? Do you? Then just who's left to blame that fellow's death on? Hilcrest? You shot at him, remember? Look what good it did. He's still here!" Wentworth's anger twisted his face. His eyes glinted daggers as they locked on the deputy.

"It was your idea, Wentworth! I say we kill him too!"

Wentworth half-stood. "You think about as much as a longhorn does before he lets himself be hazed on to a rail car bound for the slaughterhouse! Use your head, you idiot! Two more bodies mean no one to blame and Presby isn't going to let that slide. He'll be on our tails like a coyote on a rabbit."

"I'll kill him, too!" Deputy Jenson declared, thumping a fist on the desk.

"Godammit! Will you just let me do the thinking for a change? You'll dig us deeper and deeper with your blundering!"

Jenson stiffened, posture threatening. "You best be watchin' your mouth."

Wentworth drilled the deputy with his gaze, not backing down. Jenson's eyes flicked away after a tense moment and for the first time he took a step back.

"What you got in mind?" he muttered, voice lowering.

"I thought you'd see it my way." Wentworth lowered into his chair. "First we let Mr Hilcrest find the place, assuming he does."

"*What?*" Deputy Jenson bleated. "Oh my God, you are loco! Plumb fool loco!"

"Am I?" Wentworth steepled his fingers. "Say he finds it. That place is secret and no one would be likely to stumble across it again. Man could turn to bones down there."

A light dawned in Jenson's eyes, sweeping the anger away. "I see what you're aimin' at."

"Glad I don't have to spell it out for you, Jenson. If Mr Hilcrest disappears he's simply another treasure hunter who gave up and moved on to greener pastures."

Deputy Jenson smiled. "I see your point. What about the witch?"

"I've been giving her some thought. She's a different story. Town already thinks she killed that fellow with her black magic. Won't take a very big match to light a fire . . . all we need is for you to throw a little more kindlin' on it."

"How do I do that?"

"You figure it out. Hold a town meeting, work some . . . *magic*."

"Then?"

Wentworth shrugged. "Then? Why, the town has its murderer and everything just dies down. It'll be just like it was before Hilcrest arrived and stirred things up, and we can take our time getting rid of the jewels."

The smile on the deputy's face broadened and he nodded. "Maybe I should let you do the thinkin' more often." He started for the door.

"Oh, one more thing, Jenson."

"What's that?"

"There's still a weak link in the plan."

"Yeah?" Jenson's face darkened.

"Mr Hilcrest might be lonely rotting by himself. I think Deenie would make fine company for him. I hope you won't see a problem with that."

Deputy Jenson appeared to consider it and shrugged. "Well, it was nice while it lasted. Hell, everybody knows she's a gold-digging tramp anyway. No one'll miss her. Bargirls pull stakes all the time."

"Good. Now we understand each other."

"Perfectly."

★ ★ ★

"We have a wanton woman in our midst!" Deputy Jenson yelled, standing atop an over-turned crate in front of the bank. A crowd had gathered — a crowd consisting of roughly ten folks in Hags Bend — to hear him speak as soon as he made reference to the witch at the outskirts of town.

"She's a witch!" Jenson raised his fist for emphasis.

"A witch . . ." the crowd murmured. They huddled closer, faces tense, expectant. Deputy Jenson knew he just about had them. Wentworth was right: it would take damn little to get them worked into a lynching frenzy.

"She killed that poor man, Bord! Shot him dead and strung him up like he was a side of beef!

"Killed him and she'll eventually kill us all with her black magic."

"What'll we do?" a voice shouted from the crowd.

"What'll we do?" Jenson repeated, gazing back and forth over the people. "What'll we do? Why, we'll have to do what they always do to witches — burn her out!"

A cheer ululated through the crowd and fists raised.

"Burn her out!" they chanted.

"If we don't she'll take our town, kill our children." Jenson knew he was laying it on thick, but he sensed a hesitancy in the folk, despite their agreement and support. They teetered on the edge and he had to push them over. Despite their collective habit of forming instant and lopsided opinions of others, they were basically a decent lot and it took work to stir their suspicions to action.

"Do you want that?" he shouted, spreading his hands. *"Do you?"*

"NO!" the cry rang out.

"Then what do you aim to do about it?"

The murmur grew louder but no one moved.

"I said, what do you aim to do about it? Are you cowards? Are you just gonna stand by while she kills your children and takes your town and makes you all slaves of hell?"

The 'slaves of hell' routine he had read in a dime novel and he reckoned it would be the clincher here. Hags Bend was a God-fearing town, given to talk of demons and devils. Where you had a seed already planted, water it, he reckoned.

"No! Burn her out!"

The men moved. One grabbed a hanging lantern from a shop wall and the rest followed, marching through the street. Deputy Jenson smiled, entirely pleased with himself. One problem down, one — make that two with Deenie — to go.

"What the *hell* are you doin'?" A voice cracked behind him. He felt the arrogance drop from his manner. Turning, he saw Sheriff Presby stepping from his office, hat in hand. The sheriff strode towards him, hell on his face.

"Nothin'. I had a problem and I dealt with it."

The sheriff eyed the men leaving the town for the hard-packed trail. "Where they goin'?" His tone grew icy and Deputy Jenson felt himself recoil. Presby intimidated him, though he never would have admitted that to Wentworth.

"They're goin' to take care of that murderess, that witch!"

"*What?*" Presby spat, anger crashing on to his face. "What the hell have you gone and done?"

Jenson forced his shoulders back and

his voice down. "She killed Bord; now, she'll get hers."

"You're a damn sorry excuse for a lawman, Jenson. I've suspected it for a while, but now I'm sure." He tore the badge from Jenson's chest, hurling it to the dust. "You get yourself outa my sight before I decide you ain't worth the hide you were born in."

Jenson stared at Presby, debating whether to kill the sheriff on the spot, but deciding against it. Presby would prove too much for him face to face, but the nights got awfully dark in Hags Bend. Jenson's opportunity would come later and Quinton Hilcrest would have one more body to keep him company on the trail to eternity.

★ ★ ★

A knock hammered the door to his hotel room and Quinton jolted. The sound snapped him out of deep thought. Since he had left Turquoise at the cemetery, nothing else had been

210

on his mind but the lovely blue-green-eyed woman.

He went to the door, opening it. A sinking sensation hit his belly as he stared at the tense-set features of Sheriff Presby.

Presby glanced at the Peacemaker strapped to Quinton's hips. "See you got yourself a piece. Know how to use it?"

Quinton nodded. "Not well. You come here to question me about that?"

"No, I came here for your help, Hilcrest, though it pains me to admit it."

"My help?"

"That is if you want to see your lady friend live out the day."

The seriousness of the statement took Quinton aback. "You have my attention, Sheriff."

"Just caught my deputy incitin' the town against her. Least ten of 'em or so headed her way. They ain't got a welcome-to-the-community look in their eyes."

The sinking sensation became a solid knot. That cut it: Jenson was involved but he would have to worry about that later. Now, Turquoise needed his help. He grabbed his derby from the dresser and stepped out after the sheriff.

"I have a horse — "

"Already tied in front, Mr Hilcrest, next to mine."

★ ★ ★

A rock shattered a window. Turquoise, placing a kettle on the fire, started. Her thoughts had been centered on Quinton Hilcrest and the events at the cemetery. The sudden intrusion unnerved her. She dropped the kettle, splashing tea across her skirt.

"Damn," she muttered, gripping her nerves. She saw a hand-sized rock roll to a stop in front of the sofa. Outside, shouts rose and a chill swept over her.

She looked towards the window, then ran to the door, edging it open a crack, peering out. At least ten men from town, anger on their faces, paced about ten yards from the cabin. One carried a lantern and was touching a lucifer to the wick.

"What do you want?" she shouted, voice shaky. The intent was clear on their faces and she cursed them, as she had many times before. They were worse than she had ever been accused of being, folks led by silly superstitions and Dark-Age thinking.

"Get out here, witch!" one shouted. "Get out here or we'll burn you with the place!"

The man with the lantern cocked his arm and hurled it. The lantern shattered against the side of the cabin with a sharp *whoof*! The wall exploded in flame. She gasped and came out on to the porch, screeching.

"Get out of here! Get out of here, you bastards! Leave me alone!"

"You get out, witch! You got no place here no more."

She grabbed a shovel leaning against the wall and threw it at the man who'd

213

flung the lantern. It landed beside him and he laughed. She ignored him, running into the cabin. Pulling a blanket from the bed, she went back out and soaked it in the rain trough. With it, she slapped at the flames, but the task was too much for one woman. Her arms grew leaden, but she kept trying. Flame crept along the wall and she felt weighted by the futility of her effort. This was it: she would have nothing when her cabin burned; her things, her dolls, her life, all would perish and she would be abandoned, alone, more than she had ever been.

She renewed her efforts, driven by desperation. Behind her she heard the men jeering, though none made a move to stop her. They knew as well as she it was useless, that everything she had left was about to go to hell in flames.

★ ★ ★

"Looks like we're none too soon, Hilcrest," Sheriff Presby shouted as they drew up behind the crowd.

"Leave her be!" Quinton yelled, drawing his Peacemaker as the sheriff did the same.

Presby fired a shot into the air and the men turned, appearing on the verge of charging them, but thinking better of it.

"She's got to go, Sheriff!" a man fired back. "She'll kill our children."

Presby's face tightened. "Where the hell you come by that hogwash? She's no more evil than you are, Otis, but she'll be in a lot better shape than you if you don't get your ass home, now! I catch you up to something like this again and I'll put you out of commission for good!" He gestured with the .45. Quinton watched, tensing. The man named Otis made no move and Quinton climbed from his horse. He darted into the cabin, grabbing another blanket.

A murmur swelled through the crowd, but they backed off and began filtering down the trail. Presby jumped from his horse and holstered his Peacemaker. He located a blanket and helped them douse the flames. What was too much for one person proved nearly the equal of three. After dragging moments and leaden muscles, they got the fire out.

Soot smudged Turquoise's face and tears drew black lines across her cheeks. Quinton drew her close.

Damage to the cabin proved minimal but logs were blackened over a wide area and the place would reek of crisped wood for a spell.

"Thanks, Sheriff." Quinton looked at Presby. He meant his gratitude. Without Presby coming to get him, Turquoise would have been burned out of a home, possibly worse.

"Just doin' my job, Hilcrest. You opened a can of worms, here, I got to tell you, but maybe it was one that needed opening. I got the notion you both ain't on real steady legs where things in Hags Bend are concerned."

"Think they'll try again?" Quinton

nudged his head at the trail, the last of the men a distant spot.

"No, ain't likely you'll have trouble on that front. But whoever put 'em up to it — 'sides Jenson, I mean — well, that's a different story. You best stick close to the lady and get real well acquainted with that piece." He nodded at the Peacemaker on Quinton's hip, then walked to his horse.

After watching Presby ride off, Quinton looked at Turquoise, who smiled thinly. "Seems I owe you a debt of gratitude. I wonder how I can ever repay you . . ."

He grinned. "We'll think of something."

"How 'bout this?" She kissed him full and deep and he felt himself slip away in her arms. "I love you, Quinton. I should have said it earlier, but I mean it."

"That's the best news I've heard in ages." He held her close as the sky darkened to velvet and his heart out-shone the brightest star.

9

"**I** HAVE to leave, now, Quinton. I have no choice." Turquoise stood by the window, gazing out at the rising sun that splashed the fall leaves with flaming colors. Diamond sparkles glinted off the dew and steam wisped as the earth warmed. Quinton had boarded up the broken window and a high fire warded off the chill.

"Then we'll leave together." He stood from the sofa on which he'd slept. He had decided to keep an eye on her throughout the night. If trouble came again, they might not be so lucky as to have the sheriff spot it in time. The forces behind the trouble in Hags Bend had struck at Turquoise once and it was only a matter of time before they tried again. He had to beat them to the punch.

"But first I'm going to town for one

last stab at those jewels," he said. "Last night convinced me someone found the jewels and will do anything to protect them. That means getting us out of the picture."

"They aren't worth it, Quinton. You'll get yourself killed over them and I can't face another . . . death."

"I promise I'll be careful. Who knows, it may lead to nothing anyway." He tried to make his smile sincere, but the effort fell short.

"If it doesn't, promise me we'll leave just the same. I'm used to living hand to mouth and I'm used to living alone. I'll accept the first, but not the second any longer."

"I promise." He went to her, placing a hand gently on her shoulder and turning her towards him. He kissed her on the cheek and went to the door.

"Come back." Worry bled in her eyes.

"I will." He meant it. His reckless streak was slipping away. He had something — someone — now, a dream that had become reality. Suddenly his gambles needed favorable odds, but he would make a last attempt to finish what he had started. However, he would be careful.

He opened the door, pausing. "Keep your shot-gun handy. Anyone steps on that porch other than me or the sheriff, fill them with holes."

"The deputy?"

"Especially the deputy!"

Quinton rode the trail to town, dread gnawing at his being. Fear like this was a new sensation to him, that fluttery sense of worry over the way things might turn out. While he had chased dreams so many times before, never giving the outcome much thought, now he had his dream in the form of a beautiful woman who filled the hole he hadn't realized existed inside him. He felt ready to settle down anywhere, as long as she was with him and that gave him a sense of peace. At the same time it made him edgy, alert for the slightest thing to go wrong. Whoever had moved against him and Turquoise, through Jenson, would likely step things up unless Quinton tied the loose ends together quickly. But he couldn't leave just yet. He had one more windmill to chase before he gave them up for good: the jewels.

One thing Quinton felt sure of: Jenson had not acted alone. His humiliation at the hands of Presby would make the deputy as likely to sting as a wasp. Quinton would have to keep his eyes open for the former lawman while in town. But what about the man behind it all? Wentworth, Quinton was certain. How would the lawyer react to what had occurred? Quinton couldn't be sure. He guessed Wentworth would stay in the shadows, waiting for an opportunity to strike. That gave Quinton a last chance to find the jewels. If he were wrong . . . he didn't want to think about it.

What if they've already sold all the jewels?

The question invaded his thoughts.

If they had, he was risking much on a wild goose chase. But that 'scent' told him the jewels, at least a part of them, had to be nearby or Wentworth and Jenson wouldn't have gone to such an effort to stop him. That many jewels would prove hard to dispense with at a fast clip; it would attract too much attention. That still left the question of where they were hidden.

The cemetery? Quinton felt positive that was the place, especially after Bord's death and Turquoise's encounter with Jenson. But where? A piece was still missing. And if anyone knew where that piece would be, she would come in the irascible form of a newspaperwoman named Molly Malone.

Drawing up in front of the newspaper office, he dismounted and scanned the street for any sign of Jenson. His gaze settled a moment on Wentworth's office and he swallowed, more jittery than he cared to be.

He crossed the boardwalk, going into the office to find Molly at work behind the printing press. She gazed up from beneath her visor, a grin sliding onto her face.

"Top of the morning, Mr Hilcrest! Glad you could stop by again. I hear you been keeping some new company — care to give me an exclusive?"

"Ah," he said, tipping his derby, "you've been listening to rumors, Molly."

"Never put much stock in rumors, sir. Go right to the source." Molly waved a pudgy hand. "Hell, I know she ain't no witch! I'm a right good judge of character, recollect?"

Except possibly in one instance, he thought, but said, "I need a favor, Molly."

"Name it, Mr Hilcrest. Anything for a drinkin' buddy." Going to the file, she popped the flask from the drawer and passed it to him.

He took a swig, forcing a grin. "When I read the accounts of the Black Hoods' downfall, I noticed none mentioned if the surviving bandit had said anything to the sheriff before he died."

Molly scratched her head and swiped at her nose, a thoughtful expression crossing her face. "Didn't say nothin' but a string of curses, as I recollect."

That did it, then, he thought, sighing. He had just run out of options where finding the jewels was concerned. He had promised Turquoise he'd waste no more time on it and he would hold to it. That left merely going to the hotel to collect his things and leaving Hags Bend empty handed, but only in that respect. He had found something much more valuable.

"Thank you, m'dear." He tipped his hat and backed towards the door.

"I get the notion you're leavin' Hags Bend, Mr Hilcrest. You seem . . . " — she cocked an eyebrow — "*different* than the first time we met."

He smiled an easy smile. "I am different, Molly, but in a way I always wanted to be." He opened the door. "And a wasps' nest is not the best place to leave your hand after you've reached under a dark eave."

"Reckon you're right about that, Mr Hilcrest. Takes a smart man to know it, too — oh, I just recollected something."

"Yes?"

"Don't know if it's any help, but that Wentworth did say his piece just before he got his neck stretched. Trouble is, it don't make no sense."

"And what might that be, Molly?"

"He told the sheriff he could go straight to hell on angel's wings. Now that don't make no sense, does it? I mean angels and hell are opposites."

A scene flashed into Quinton's mind: the cemetery. His eyes brightened.

"On the contrary, Molly. It makes perfect sense and in this case you'd need an angel to get to hell." He closed the door, leaving Molly with a perplexed expression.

★ ★ ★

225

Deputy Jenson watched Quinton Hilcrest leave the newspaper office and mount his horse. He pressed close to the wall at the corner of the building, keeping out of sight. He had been on his way to Wentworth's office when he saw the door open and Hilcrest say something to the newspaper woman. So Hilcrest was still in town, even after the little scare put into the witch woman. Quinton Hilcrest was a stubborn sort, one who didn't know when to take friendly advice. That made no never mind to him, no it didn't. In fact, he'd hoped the detective would ignore the warnings, the witch, too. Now he was free to clean up the mess permanently. If it weren't for them he'd still have his job. Not that that mattered particularly to him, but it made things easier. As soon as he had dispensed with the jewels he would have put lead in Presby's belly anyway. Now things had to be stepped up.

Jenson stayed close to the wall until he saw Hilcrest exit the hotel with a bag and secure it to his horse. The detective cast a wary look about as he mounted and Deputy Jenson stepped back, making sure he couldn't be seen. At the sound of hoofbeats he peered around the corner, seeing the detective ride down the trail. He could only be headed two places, though it occurred to Jenson if Hilcrest had packed his bag he intended leaving Hags Bend. Jenson had to move fast or lose his chance.

He walked around the corner, going to Wentworth's office. Wentworth looked up as he came in, an irritated expression drawing his lips tight.

"What the hell do you want?"

"Hilcrest is headed up to the cemetery," Jenson lied, picking the location that suited him best. "He just got done talking to that newspaper woman and I think she told him where the jewels are."

"That's impossible; she doesn't know," insisted Wentworth, waving his hand.

"Yeah? If she told him what she told us it wouldn't be too big a step from there for him to figure it out."

"You sure?" Wentworth's face darkened.

"Damn right I'm sure! I say we clean this up right now, take care of both of 'em 'fore it's too late."

Wentworth sighed, considering the words. "You may be right this time."

"Hell, course I'm right! Your little plan to take care of that witch didn't exactly work, did it?" The deputy drilled him with a look of fury.

"All right, deal with them. They'll both disappear like the Black Hoods, then we'll be done with them for good."

"What about Malone and Deenie?"

Wentworth shook his head. "Don't like it. It's adding up to too many vanishings at once. The sheriff — "

"I'll take care of him right along with the rest. Who's gonna question it after that?"

Wentworth frowned, gaze narrowing. "Hilcrest and the woman are my most immediate concern. Take care of them for now. We'll discuss the rest later."

Jenson's face reddened. "This time the discussin's over. I ain't too sure I aim to take your orders no more. Maybe it's time you followed mine."

"See here — " Wentworth half-stood, posture rigid.

"No, you see here!" Jenson cut him off. "I didn't come here for your approval. I came to tell you things are gonna be different!"

"You need me."

"Yeah, I do, to fence those jewels. Way I see it, we need each other. But from now on there's gonna be a shift in partnership control. I'll give the orders and you'll handle your end like always."

Wentworth settled back into his chair, fury shining like skulls in his eyes. After a strained moment, the squirrelly look to his features strengthened and the fury receded. "Very well, Jenson. I'll take your lead. But you'd best watch how you talk to me in the future. I'm not likely to be so patient . . . do we understand each other?"

Jenson grinned. "Yeah, we understand each other just fine."

★ ★ ★

After Deputy Jenson had left, Wentworth gazed out of the window for long moments, thoughts lost in fury and consideration. Jenson had stepped over the line and now something had to be done about him. He refused to take treatment like that from anyone. As soon as Jenson cleared up the mess . . .

Wentworth leaned forward, pulling open a drawer and locating a Smith & Wesson. He checked the chambers, making sure they were full and buckled on a gunbelt he took from a bottom drawer. Standing, he slid the revolver into its holster.

The body count in Hags Bend was climbing high, but it would notch one more after he was finished. All the loose ends would be cleaned up, including one named Jenson.

Chuck-a-luck peered out the saloon door, a worried turn to his lips. He had been on his way to the saloon when he spotted Deputy Jenson sneaking around a corner, watching something down the street. Chuck-a-luck had hung back and spotted the object of Jenson's attention: Quinton Hilcrest. Chuck-a-luck had kept an eye peeled while Jenson watched the detective ride off, then scoot into Wentworth's office, only to come out ride in the direction Hilcrest had taken moments later. That meant no good. That meant this time they would not bother firing a warning shot; they would kill Quinton Hilcrest.

Galldamn, he had told that young fella he was takin' too big a gamble. If there was somethin' Chuck-a-luck knew it was gambles. And now it looked as if the detective had rolled snake eyes — unless Chuck-a-luck could do something about it. He considered the problem a moment, knowing if his plan didn't work his life wouldn't be worth a confederate bank note. But what choice did he have? He had always taken the gamble and he was too damn old to change.

With a deep breath, he stepped out of the saloon and scooted down the boardwalk to the sheriff's office. He went in and Presby looked up, cocking an eyebrow.

"Mighty early for you to be payin' a visit, ain't it?" Presby said.

"I got a notion there's all hell about to break, Sheriff, trouble for Mr Hilcrest and that witch woman."

Presby groaned. "Tell me somethin' I don't know already!"

Chuck-a-luck explained what he had seen and, as the sheriff listened, his expression grew serious.

"Damn!" Presby stood and checked his Peacemaker's chamber. "I knew it would come to this if Hilcrest didn't pull stakes. You'd think that close call last night would have convinced him of such."

"We goin' after Jenson, then?"

"I aim to. I don't know what this is all about, but I want some answers and Jenson's gonna give 'em to me. Stay here." He jabbed a finger at Chuck-a-luck and gripped the door handle. "They come back here, you come get me, you hear?"

Chuck-a-luck nodded and the sheriff stepped out. Chuck-a-luck went to the window and watched the lawman ride away. He was about to leave for the saloon when he saw a door open down the street. Norvell Wentworth stepped out, sun glinting from the Smith & Wesson at his hip. That was new; Chuck-a-luck had never seen the lawyer carry a piece before. He watched as Wentworth walked to the livery and secured a horse, then set out after the sheriff.

"Godalmighty! We're havin' us a busy morning," he muttered, a sinking sensation in his belly. The sheriff had told him to stay here, but the lawman hadn't reckoned on being dogged by

Wentworth, who obviously saw fit to take matters into his own hands. That left Chuck-a-luck with little choice. He had to take another gamble, perhaps the biggest of his life, and follow Wentworth. Lives depended on it and this time he hoped the dice would roll his way.

10

SHE wished Quinton would return. As the hour passed she grew more and more worried. If something happened to him . . .

She refused to think about it. He was fine. He had discovered a lead to the jewels' whereabouts and was collecting them at this very moment. Then they would ride away to live happily ever after. Wasn't that the way it worked out in books?

The gnawing dread in her belly told her things seldom worked that way in real life. Too many independent factors were at work. Too much was at stake. And she was too used to losing her loved ones to place much faith in happy endings.

A muffled beating of hooves sounded outside and her hopes rose. She rushed to the window, but saw nothing. It puzzled her. Whoever it had been had ridden right past the cabin. The only thing in that direction was the cemetery.

As she went back to the sofa, her dread deepened, though she couldn't be sure why. Was it Quinton? Had he discovered where the jewels were hidden in the cemetery, if they were there at all?

Another sound pulled her from her thoughts. Hoofbeats again, cut suddenly short. Maybe —

Heavy footfalls clomped across the porch and her heart lurched. It wasn't Quinton; whoever it was wore boots.

She gained her feet, glancing at the shot-gun resting on the kitchen table and took a step towards it.

A blast jolted her in mid-step. The front door lock splintered. The door bounded inward, kicked open. A man filled the doorway, face leering, eyes touched with insanity. He leveled a Colt at her and she considered leaping for the shot-gun, knowing she'd never make it before he gunned her down.

"Wouldn't if'n I were you, witch!" Deputy Jenson stepped into the cabin, waving the Colt threateningly. "It'd just make your death all the quicker."

"What do you want?" she shot back, fighting to keep her voice steady.

"We're gonna take us a little walk, you an' me, meet your boyfriend up at the cemetery. Then you an' him can spend the rest of eternity together . . ."

★ ★ ★

Quinton drew the bay to a stop and dismounted. Tethering the animal to an iron rail, he walked into the cemetery. Molly's words made no sense to her, but they made perfect sense to him — more than likely they had made sense to Deputy Jenson or Norvell Wentworth as well. The younger Wentworth had left a mocking clue to the jewels' whereabouts before dying, one the sheriff never suspected. The sheriff was a good lawman but not a detective.

Quinton was convinced the clue had been left for Norvell Wentworth, whom Calvin had known would come seeking the jewels.

Quinton paused, the hairs prickling on the nape of his neck. All the way from town a feeling of being watched had plagued him, since he had left Molly's in fact. He had spotted no one, but the feeling wouldn't leave him. Along with it, he felt a moving urgency. Time was running out and he had to act quickly if he and Turquoise were going to have those jewels and escape with their lives.

He drew his Peacemaker, hefted it, getting the weapon's feel in case he had to use it. He prayed he'd have a bigger target than a bottle if he had to use it. He slipped the gun back into the holster.

Moving deeper into the cemetery, he halted at the base of the huge marble angel.

"To hell on angel wings," he muttered, peering at the statue. The answer had been staring him in the face all the time. The secret of the Black Hoods' vanishings, the secret of the jewels. Before he had given the statue no more than a glance; now, studying it closely, running his fingertips along the edges, he located a hairline crack on one side. Even looking for it the crack would prove difficult to find. Anyone not knowing would pass it off as a flaw in the workmanship. He stepped back, surveying the angel. He had found the answer but it would do him little good if he couldn't get in.

Angel wings . . .

He leaped, catching the edge of the base and swinging a leg up. Standing atop the base, he reached up and probed behind the left wing of the angel, then the right.

A catch! He slid the catch left and the base grated open beneath his feet. Jumping down, he saw a stone door had slid inward on some sort of pulley arrangement he didn't understand. He peered into the opening, which was large enough to take a horse. Wide stone steps led downward.

"Very good, Hilcrest, you did put it together."

Quinton whirled, ice pooling in his belly. Behind him stood Deputy Jenson, holding Turquoise in front of him as a shield. He had the Colt jammed to her temple.

"Jenson!" Fury stirred in Quinton at the sight of the helpless girl.

"You are to be congratulated, Hilcrest. Took me and Wentworth a good month to figure out what the angel wing thing meant. Don't worry, though, I'll make sure Molly doesn't let anyone else in on our little secret, 'specially since you'll be carryin' it with you to the grave."

"You've gotten a lot more talkative since the first time we met."

"I like to gloat. Now, if you'd be so kind as to drop your gunbelt." He thumbed back the hammer on his Colt.

"Don't, Quinton! Let him kill me, not both of us!"

Quinton eyed Turquoise, then the deputy swallowing hard. He was suddenly sorry he had holstered the Peacemaker. "No, I said we'd leave together and I meant it." He reached down, unbuckling the belt and letting it drop to the ground.

Jenson laughed and shoved Turquoise towards him. "There's a lantern hangin' just inside the doorway. Get it."

Quinton complied, reaching in and pulling out the lantern.

"Here." Jenson tossed him a box of lucifers and Quinton lit the wick. "Now, if you'll just — "

A shot boomed. Jenson's body went suddenly stiff, face bloodless. His mouth dropped open and a snake of blood slithered out. He pitched forward, face-first into the dead leaves.

Quinton let out the breath he'd been holding. Behind the deputy stood Sheriff Presby, gun smoking.

"Chuck-a-luck told me you two might be in trouble. Reckon now we know what became of the jewels and who was behind it."

"Not totally, Sheriff," said Quinton. "There's still — "

"Norvell Wentworth," a voice finished from the edge of the woods. The sheriff turned, gun swinging. Another blast and a starburst of crimson splattered the sheriff's shoulder. The Peacemaker flew from his grip.

Norvell Wentworth stepped from behind an oak and came towards them.

"Noticed a couple of horses hitched at your place, ma'am," he said to Turquoise. "Thought I'd see what the commotion was all about."

Presby groaned, holding his shoulder. His gaze flicked towards his gun and Wentworth caught the intent.

"Over there with them, Sheriff, unless you want to die right now." Wentworth motioned with his gun.

The sheriff moved to Turquoise and Quinton, disgust mixing with the pain on his face.

"In the end you did me a favor, you

know that? I was going to eliminate Jenson anyway. He was much too hot-headed, you see. No eye for the plan, no patience for it either. Men like that, well, men like that end up dead. You might say the same for yourself, Mr Hilcrest."

"How's that?" Quinton asked.

"If you had heeded our warning you and the lady here might have enjoyed a long life together. Now . . . " He gazed at Turquoise. "The town never wanted you here, anyway; your death won't make a difference. Presby, well, that might get some notice, but when no body turns up it'll die down soon enough. And don't worry, you'll get more company later." Wentworth chuckled, not elaborating.

The lawyer stepped towards them, forcing them backward with a motion of his gun. "Down."

Quinton went first, holding the lantern in front of them. Turquoise and the sheriff followed, Wentworth taking the rear. The stairs descended to a wide passage into a chamber below the ground. A small table stood at room center, a strongbox resting atop. The vault stank of mold and dampness.

"The jewels?" Quinton asked, indicating the strongbox.

"And then some. What you see before you, Mr Hilcrest, is the secret of the Black Hoods. When they discovered this little hidey-hole, they hit upon their scheme. It was the perfect hideout. No one in Hags Bend remembered it being here. Reckon it was used by some of the early settlers when Blackfeet raided. Thanks to Molly we found it, too. The jewels, some odd cash, all of it was here waiting for us to collect. Cash was no problem, but the jewels, they have to be disposed of more carefully. We've been fencing it slowly, a diamond here, a ruby there . . . it was working fine until you blundered along."

"Sorry to be such a bother," Quinton quipped, fear making him flippant.

"A short-lived bother — " Wentworth suddenly jumped forward, slamming into Presby and bowling the sheriff over. Quinton immediately saw the reason: Chuck-a-luck stood behind the lawyer, hands outstretched.

Wentworth recovered from the shove quickly but the sheriff pitched backward, crashing on to the stone floor.

Quinton grabbed Turquoise, whirling her out of the way, dived for Wentworth.

Wentworth fought to get his gun levelled as Quinton fell on him, swinging a fist. The fist hit Wentworth's jaw with the sound of blocks colliding. Wentworth, though the bigger man, stuttered in his step.

The blow stopped Wentworth only an instant. He swung the gun in a choppy arc. Quinton jerked his head to avoid the blow, but the gunbutt clacked from his jaw in a glancing hit. He reeled, going back and down, rolling onto his belly, groaning.

"No!" Turquoise screamed, diving at Wentworth. Chuck-a-luck moved at the same time.

Wentworth lashed out with a

backhand, catching Turquoise full across the face and propelling her backward into Chuck-a-luck. They stumbled, went down, and Wentworth bellowed a laugh, swiping blood from his lip.

"It's over!" he yelled, swinging his gun on Quinton, who was pushing up, hand in a pocket.

Wentworth drew back the hammer and aimed.

A shot sounded, echoing from the walls of the chamber.

Wentworth's finger spasmed on the trigger, but his grip was already faltering. The gun dipped and the bullet ricocheted, chipping stone from the floor. Wentworth's eyes went wide. The lawyer fell forward, a hole over his heart.

Quinton gained his feet, a smoking derringer in his palm. He forced a nervous smile. "Pretty good for a lady's gun, I'd say." He eyed Chuck-a-luck, who was helping Turquoise to her feet.

"Pretty good for a fella who couldn't hit a damn bottle!" Chuck-a-luck said. "Hell, for once no one rolled snake eyes!"

* * *

"What you intend to do, Hilcrest? You, too, Miss Turquoise?" Sheriff Presby asked, tipping his hat. A sling bound his left arm. They stood outside the Weeping Willow — Quinton, Turquoise, Presby and Chuck-a-luck — awaiting the noon stage.

"With the reward from those jewels I figure we can start someplace in style. We were thinking of back East, now that I don't have to prove myself to anyone."

"You never did, Hilcrest. Only one you got to worry about is yourself and your lady here, no one else."

Quinton nodded. "I know that now. And I'm ready for it. We were thinking New York, maybe, so Turquoise can be close to the shops that sell her dolls."

"New York it is, then." Presby smiled.

Chuck-a-luck slapped a hand on Quinton's shoulder. "Gonna miss you, son. For a spell you brought some life to this town."

"And death." A somber note laced Quinton's voice. "I got more than I bargained for, that's for sure."

"Sometimes that happens when you gamble on dreams." Chuck-a-luck winked.

"He's dead right, Hilcrest!" a voice shouted behind them. "Sometimes you get what you got comin' when you destroy other folks' dreams!"

They turned in unison to see Deenie stepping from the saloon. Before anyone could move, the bargirl reached into her bodice and plucked out a derringer, aiming it at Quinton.

Chuck-a-luck and the sheriff made a move towards her, but not in time.

The derringer spat. Quinton bounded backwards, crashing to his back on the boardwalk. Turquoise screamed. A rush of footsteps sounded as Chuck-a-luck and the sheriff jumped on Deenie, who fought them like a wildcat.

By the time they subdued her, both men had scratched faces and bloody lips. The sheriff snatched the peashooter from her grip and shoved it in a pocket. They hauled the bargirl up, Chuck-a-luck finally clomping her with the back of his hand to stop her from cursing and spitting and biting.

Turquoise ran to Quinton, who lay sprawled on the boardwalk. She lifted his head, tears in her eyes.

Quinton forced a pained grin and muttered, "I think it stopped for good this time."

"What?" Turquoise's voice trembled with relief that he was still alive.

He fumbled in a pocket and brought out his watch, which had a small bullet lodged in it.

TOP HAND
Wade Everett

The Broken T was big. But no ranch is big enough to let a man hide from himself.

GUN WOLVES OF LOBO BASIN
Lee Floren

The Feud was a blood debt. When Smoke Talbot found the outlaws who gunned down his folks he aimed to nail their hide to the barn door.

SHOTGUN SHARKEY
Marshall Grover

The westbound coach carrying the indomitable Larry and Stretch headed for a shooting showdown.

FIGHTING RAMROD
Charles N. Heckelmann

Most men would have cut their losses, but Frazer counted the bullets in his guns and said he'd soak the range in blood before he'd give up another inch of what was his.

LONE GUN
Eric Allen

Smoke Blackbird had been away too long. The Lequires had seized the Blackbird farm, forcing the Indians and settlers off, and no one seemed willing to fight! He had to fight alone.

THE THIRD RIDER
Barry Cord

Mel Rawlins wasn't going to let anything stand in his way. His father was murdered, his two brothers gone. Now Mel rode for vengeance.

ARIZONA DRIFTERS
W. C. Tuttle

When drifting Dutton and Lonnie Steelman decide to become partners they find that they have a common enemy in the formidable Thurston brothers.

TOMBSTONE
Matt Braun

Wells Fargo paid Luke Starbuck to outgun the silver-thieving stagecoach gang at Tombstone. Before long Luke can see the only thing bearing fruit in this eldorado will be the gallows tree.

HIGH BORDER RIDERS
Lee Floren

Buckshot McKee and Tortilla Joe cut the trail of a border tough who was running Mexican beef into Texas. They stopped the smuggler in his tracks.

BRETT RANDALL, GAMBLER
E. B. Mann

Larry Day had the choice of running away from the law or of assuming a dead man's place. No matter what he decided he was bound to end up dead.

THE GUNSHARP
William R. Cox

The Eggerleys weren't very smart. They trained their sights on Will Carney and Arizona's biggest blood bath began.

THE DEPUTY OF SAN RIANO
Lawrence A. Keating and
Al. P. Nelson

When a man fell dead from his horse, Ed Grant was spotted riding away from the scene. The deputy sheriff rode out after him and came up against everything from gunfire to dynamite.

FARGO: MASSACRE RIVER
John Benteen

The ambushers up ahead had now blocked the road. Fargo's convoy was a jumble, a perfect target for the insurgents' weapons!

SUNDANCE: DEATH IN THE LAVA
John Benteen

The Modoc's captured the wagon train and its cargo of gold. But now the halfbreed they called Sundance was going after it . . .

HARSH RECKONING
Phil Ketchum

Five years of keeping himself alive in a brutal prison had made Brand tough and careless about who he gunned down . . .

FARGO: PANAMA GOLD
John Benteen

With foreign money behind him, Buckner was going to destroy the Panama Canal before it could be completed. Fargo's job was to stop Buckner.

FARGO:
THE SHARPSHOOTERS
John Benteen

The Canfield clan, thirty strong were raising hell in Texas. Fargo was tough enough to hold his own against the whole clan.

PISTOL LAW
Paul Evan Lehman

Lance Jones came back to Mustang for just one thing — revenge! Revenge on the people who had him thrown in jail.

HELL RIDERS
Steve Mensing

Wade Walker's kid brother, Duane, was locked up in the Silver City jail facing a rope at dawn. Wade was a ruthless outlaw, but he was smart, and he had vowed to have his brother out of jail before morning!

DESERT OF THE DAMNED
Nelson Nye

The law was after him for the murder of a marshal — a murder he didn't commit. Breen was after him for revenge — and Breen wouldn't stop at anything . . . blackmail, a frameup . . . or murder.

DAY OF THE COMANCHEROS
Steven C. Lawrence

Their very name struck terror into men's hearts — the Comancheros, a savage army of cutthroats who swept across Texas, leaving behind a bloodstained trail of robbery and murder.

SUNDANCE: SILENT ENEMY
John Benteen

A lone crazed Cheyenne was on a personal war path. They needed to pit one man against one crazed Indian. That man was Sundance.

LASSITER
Jack Slade

Lassiter wasn't the kind of man to listen to reason. Cross him once and he'll hold a grudge for years to come — if he let you live that long.

LAST STAGE TO GOMORRAH
Barry Cord

Jeff Carter, tough ex-riverboat gambler, now had himself a horse ranch that kept him free from gunfights and card games. Until Sturvesant of Wells Fargo showed up.

McALLISTER ON THE COMANCHE CROSSING
Matt Chisholm

The Comanche, McAllister owes them a life — and the trail is soaked with the blood of the men who had tried to outrun them before.

QUICK-TRIGGER COUNTRY
Clem Colt

Turkey Red hooked up with Curly Bill Graham's outlaw crew. But wholesale murder was out of Turk's line, so when range war flared he bucked the whole border gang alone . . .

CAMPAIGNING
Jim Miller

Ambushed on the Santa Fe trail, Sean Callahan is saved by two Indian strangers. But there'll be more lead and arrows flying before the band join Kit Carson against the Comanches.

GUNSLINGER'S RANGE
Jackson Cole

Three escaped convicts are out for revenge. They won't rest until they put a bullet through the head of the dirty snake who locked them behind bars.

RUSTLER'S TRAIL
Lee Floren

Jim Carlin knew he would have to stand up and fight because he had staked his claim right in the middle of Big Ike Outland's best grass.

THE TRUTH ABOUT SNAKE RIDGE
Marshall Grover

The troubleshooters came to San Cristobal to help the needy. For Larry and Stretch the turmoil began with a brawl and then an ambush.

WOLF DOG RANGE
Lee Floren

Will Ardery would stop at nothing, unless something stopped him first — like a bullet from Pete Manly's gun.

DEVIL'S DINERO
Marshall Grover

Plagued by remorse, a rich old reprobate hired the Texas Troubleshooters to deliver a fortune in greenbacks to each of his victims.

GUNS OF FURY
Ernest Haycox

Dane Starr, alias Dan Smith, wanted to close the door on his past and hang up his guns, but people wouldn't let him.

DONOVAN
Elmer Kelton

Donovan was supposed to be dead. Uncle Joe Vickers had fired off both barrels of a shotgun into the vicious outlaw's face as he was escaping from jail. Now Uncle Joe had been shot — in just the same way.

CODE OF THE GUN
Gordon D. Shirreffs

MacLean came riding home, with saddle tramp written all over him, but sewn in his shirt-lining was an Arizona Ranger's star.

GAMBLER'S GUN LUCK
Brett Austen

Gamblers seldom live long. Parker was a hell of a gambler. It was his life — or his death . . .

ORPHAN'S PREFERRED
Jim Miller

Sean Callahan answers the call of the Pony Express and fights Indians and outlaws to get the mail through.

DAY OF THE BUZZARD
T. V. Olsen

All Val Penmark cared about was getting the men who killed his wife.

THE MANHUNTER
Gordon D. Shirreffs

Lee Kershaw knew that every Rurale in the territory was on the lookout for him. But the offer of $5,000 in gold to find five small pieces of leather was too good to turn down.

RIFLES ON THE RANGE
Lee Floren

Doc Mike and the farmer stood there alone between Smith and Watson. There was this moment of stillness, and then the roar would start. And somebody would die . . .

HARTIGAN
Marshall Grover

Hartigan had come to Cornerstone to die. He chose the time and the place, and Main Street became a battlefield.

SUNDANCE: OVERKILL
John Benteen

When a wealthy banker's daughter was kidnapped by the Cheyenne, he offered Sundance $10,000 to rescue the girl.

RIDE A LONE TRAIL
Gordon D. Shirreffs

The valley was about to explode into open range war. All it needed was the fuse and Ken Macklin was it.

HARD MAN WITH A GUN
Charles N. Heckelmann

After Bob Keegan lost the girl he loved and the ranch he had sweated blood to build, he had nothing left but his guts and his guns but he figured that was enough.

SUNDANCE: IRON MEN
Peter McCurtin

Sundance, assigned to save the railroad from a murder spree, soon came to realise that he'd have to fight fire with fire, bullets with bullets and death with death!